TRABLER TRAVEL TALES

AS

OUTPOURED BY AN INSIDER

by

Walt McConville

National Library of Canada Cataloguing in Publication

McConville, Walt, 1914-
    Trabler travel tales / Walt McConville.

ISBN 1-55369-710-3

    I. Title.

PS8575.C663T72 2002   C813'.54   C2002-903198-2
PR199.3.M2938T72 2002

TRAFFORD

This book was published *on-demand* in cooperation with Trafford Publishing.
On-demand publishing is a unique process and service of making a book available for retail sale to the public taking advantage of on-demand manufacturing and Internet marketing.
On-demand publishing includes promotions, retail sales, manufacturing, order fulfilment, accounting and collecting royalties on behalf of the author.

Suite 6E, 2333 Government St., Victoria, B.C. V8T 4P4, CANADA

Phone	250-383-6864	Toll-free	1-888-232-4444 (Canada & US)
Fax	250-383-6804	E-mail	sales@trafford.com
Web site	www.trafford.com	TRAFFORD PUBLISHING IS A DIVISION OF TRAFFORD HOLDINGS LTD.
Trafford Catalogue #02-0523		www.trafford.com/robots/02-0523.html

10   9   8   7   6   5   4   3   2   1

DEDICATION

To my colleagues in travel,

my fellow authors,

my many loyal clients

and suppliers

IN GENERAL

and to my daughter

Marjorie Ellen ("Midge")

who contributed the Right Word

at the Right Time

IN PARTICULAR

OTHER PUBLICATIONS BY THE AUTHOR

Books: *Talara by Teaspoon*, Primrose Press, 1992

Anxious in Talara, Trafford Publishing, 2000

Fiery Facets, Trafford Publishing, 2002

Editorials, short stories, poetry, travel and technical articles in

The Beaver, Calgary Herald, Canadian Author,

The Canadian Writer's Guide (13th edition), El Fanal,

El Noticiero Talareño, The Gregg Writer, Orbis International

Quarterly, Saanich News, South Hill Pioneer, Times Colonist,

Trillium Books, WestWorld, Winners' Circle Short Stories 1997;

edited and published *Victoria Calling* (CAA branch newsletter),

wrote, directed and staged two historical plays in 1979 & 1980,

and three musicals in 1993, 1995 and 1997.

--o-O-o--

CONTENTS

TRABLER TRAVEL TALES

by

Walt McConville

TRABLER ABETS A CLASSIFIED COURTSHIP

"Cinco más cuatro por nueve menos uno entre ocho*" was the problem I put to my Spanish class. *"¿Cuánto son?"*

Several hands shot up and I chose one from the third row.

"¡Señor Jackson!"

"Son diez, señor profesor," Glen Jackson answered correctly, with a triumphant sweep of eyes over his classmates.

I, Terry Trabler, employed by a Calgary travel agency in the 1960s, supplemented my meagre income by instructing conversational Spanish classes at Mount Royal College three nights each week. My students were mainly middle-agers who had visited or intended visiting Hispanic countries, so they were goal-oriented. They studied industriously, eager-beavered their homework, and peppered me with pertinent questions. It was a joy to teach them.

These classes were entirely in Spanish, and one of my ploys for stimulating their thinking in that language was by practicing numerical calculations in it. We gradually accelerated the speed until there was no time for tedious translation. The only way to keep pace was by relentlessly forcing oneself to concentrate.

* For translations, see Glossary at end of book

Later we spelled Spanish words, but in the *Spanish* alphabet. When travelling in another land, one cannot expect its people to spell an unfamiliar word in *English*, right? So our theme was enjoyment and learning was fun. Smiling at each others' errors helped sweeten the pill by reducing embarrassment.

Besides middle-aged students, there were young ones who contemplated a career in Latin America, and some who came for various personal reasons. These included Glen Jackson, a handsome young fellow already mentioned.

Glen had taken a vacation in Mexico during which he met an attractive *tapatía* from Guadalajara named Vituca. Vituca (Latin nickname for "Victoria"), a University student, on her free days functioned as a multilingual tour guide at Mexico's National Museum of Anthropology in Chapultepec Park. The museum tour was a portion of Glen's vacation package, and Vituca just happened to be on duty the day his group visited.

"This huge calendar stone," she told them as they entered the spectacular Aztec hall, "weighs 27 metric tons and is more accurate than European calendars of the same period." She interpreted some of its pictographs, and then escorted the group to other halls filled with exotic relics from the Mayan, Toltec, Mixtec, Zapotec and Tarascan cultures. Glen was fascinated by the imposing exhibits and even more by curvaceous, vivacious Vituca. Her tour alone, in his estimation, was worth the price of the trip.

The lunch break following the first half of the tour was at the fabulous *Restaurante del Lago* by the Natural History Museum. Glen wangled a seat at the same table as Vituca, but found that her English vocabulary was confined to tour information. Still, although Glen's Spanish was minimal, their conversation soon became animated and enjoyable. Unluckily, it was interrupted.

An Ecuadorian tourist at an adjacent table began questioning Vituca, in rapid Spanish, about some of the museum's artifacts. Vituca politely excused herself to Glen while she dealt with the man, and Glen realized that his own deficiency in the language put him in the outfield. Moreover, the Ecuadorian's romantic demeanor galvanized Glen to a subconscious reflex of jealousy which shocked and surprised him.

This was ridiculous, he told himself. Why, he hardly knew the girl and she was only doing her job. Nevertheless, he had to admit she had a lot going for her and he had never known anyone quite like her. Also, from the way she glanced at him every so often, he surmised that the feeling was mutual -- that she rather liked what she saw in this young *canadiense.*

Anyway, before the tour was over Vituca had made a deal with Glen that "you to me shall write in Espanish and I to you in *Inglés* and by correcting from each other we learn, yes?"

On his return to Calgary, then, Glen enrolled in my class at Mount Royal as he now had a definite incentive. I agreed to assist with his amorous correspondence provided that he made the initial effort. He would phrase his own ideas and I would make suggestions for improving the raw material, so to speak. Regardless of temptation in no way would I put my words into his mouth or on his paper. That would spoil the spontaneity of his outpourings, I explained, or might seriously impair the out-come of this rather intimate enterprise.

The exchange of letters began innocently enough, but soon

reached beyond mere courtesy. First there were hints of deeper sentiment, then suggestions of a common future, and eventually bold broad statements of heartfelt longing between those two.

There were times when I was frankly embarrassed by things they wrote to each other, and at one crucial stage I almost withdrew to leave them to their own resources.

Vituca had been pressuring Glen to make a brief return trip to Mexico to meet her family. "I feel from our letters I now know you *concienzudamente,*" she wrote, "and *mi corazón* tells me there is no other person *con quien* I rather would share the rest of my life. But Glen *querido,* it would mean so much to me to have the blessing of *mi familia,* to know that they concur with my high esteem for you, and that we are so right for each other, *¿entiendes?*"

"I think I'd better book a flight down there, over the Labour Day weekend," Glen said in my office, showing me this latest piece of correspondence. "Could you find me a cheap excursion airfare that won't cost me an arm and a leg?" He was obviously flattered by young Vituca's unabashed affirmation, and I had no desire to deflate his euphoria at that point.

"Right," I agreed. "is your passport still current?"

"Good for another two years," he assured me.

"Fine. I'll check the flight availability for that holiday weekend and phone you once I have something lined up. It may take several tries, since we don't have too much lead-in time before the actual travel date, or flights may be overbooked. Just out of curiosity, Glen, how has your own family reacted to all this?"

"Well, so far they haven't given me any flak. But they're in West Vancouver, you know. We don't correspond that much. In a phone conversation with Dad several weeks ago he sort of took my interest in Vituca as a mere infatuation which distance would eventually destroy. In fact, he quoted Mother as wondering why I wasn't courting a *Canadian* girl."

"There's no accounting for the quarry of Cupid's quiver," I mused, "and I know from our dealings that your intentions are above board. So by all means feel free to come to me for whatever further assistance you may require."

"Thanks, Mr. Trabler. You've already performed miracles in rubbing the rough edges off my Spanish!" He departed in good spirits and I got on the phone to the airlines.

Two days later a despondent Glen Jackson handed me an airmail envelope bearing Mexican stamps. "What am I supposed to do about **this**?" he asked. I extracted the letter and gasped.

It was a single sheet of featherweight notepaper bearing the terse typewritten message: *"Deje de estorbar a Victoria. Ella pertenece a otro más meritorio."* Translated it cautioned "Stop interfering with Victoria. She belongs to someone much more deserving." Naturally, there was no signature.

"Well!" I exclaimed."Looks like you've raised some hackles. Any idea who it might be?"

"None whatever. We've been writing each other for several months now, with never an indication of hidden rivalry."

"It's probably a good idea that you're going down there in a short while," I suggested. "Hopefully you'll get to the bottom of this harrowing situation."

"But, how could such a thing be?" said Glen incredulously. "Just when everything was going so wonderfully well."

"That's life,"I told him. "Whenever we take good fortune for granted some obstacle compels us to look more closely at it in order to strengthen our resolve."

"Maybe so. But this cowardly skulduggery hits below the belt. And there's no way of tracking it down."

"For that very reason, Glen, I wouldn't attach too much importance to it. If there were any legitimacy in their grudge they wouldn't have to hide behind a sneaky stratagem."

"You're probably right, Mr. Trabler. I'll try to erase it from my mind then, but you must admit it's unsettling."

- - - - -

When Glen had returned from his weekend journey I was anxious to hear what he had found out, but he had nothing to report regarding the anonymous missive.

"Did you mention it to Vituca?" I asked.

"I did eventually," he admitted. "She thought it a prank by her younger brother Pablito, but he denied any knowledge of it when confronted."

"How did you get along with her parents?"

"First rate, thanks. The family home is in Guadalajara, you know. They have a big house by the Country Club on Avenida Monte Casino, not too far from the main hospital. Vituca's dad is a physician and her mother works for the hospital office. On one occasion we dined at the posh *La Fuente* restaurant close to their home. The international cuisine was splendid."

"So how is the romance progressing?"

"Fine, fine. Vituca will be graduated from the university by next spring and we hope to be married shortly thereafter."

"And your folks are in complete agreement?"

"Well, actually, I still have to work things out on my own home front in the very near future. Could you please book me a return flight to Vancouver during Thanksgiving week?"

"That shouldn't be too difficult, Glen. If you depart on the Thursday and return the following Tuesday I'll fix you up with a reasonably-priced seat-sale fare, depending on availability."

"Great. I'll leave the details up to you, Mr. Trabler."

"No problem; I'll phone you when the flight's confirmed."

- - - - -

Glen went to Vancouver for the Thanksgiving holiday, and a month later I received a wedding invitation from his parents. The accompanying note explained that my name was on the guest list because of my assistance with the classified courtship by correspondence. The wedding and reception would be held

at the home of Glen's parents in West Vancouver, an address in
a wealthy area known as British Properties.

I flew out to the Coast in time for the occasion, and Glen's
mother and father treated me like a long-lost relative. Glen had
flown to Guadalajara to escort Vituca and family to Vancouver,
so Mr. and Mrs. Jackson took me along to meet them at the airport. Vituca's brother Pablito carried a clipboard with sheets of
lightweight notepaper on which he had been sketching portraits
of passengers aboard the plane. Pablito had talent; the sketches
were extremely well done and he was justifiably proud of them.

Vituca was a real charmer and I could see how Glen had been
swept off his feet. It was not long before she had the rest of us
under her spell also. Her striking looks, engaging manner and
spontaneous laughter made her an instant hit with people. Her
parents spoke halting English but, with polite help from Vituca,
Glen and myself, the conversation flowed freely enough.

"Let's have lunch at Pancho's," Glen suggested on the way back
from the airport. "It's a popular Mexican café just off Granville
where they serve the best *guacamole* in town."

"Sounds okay to me, son," agreed his dad. "How do the rest
of you feel? Shall we go to Pancho's?"

Vituca and her parents nodded their assent, but Pablito was
none too enthusiastic. We learned later that he had been hoping
to sample a McDonald's during his visit to Canada. Also, Glen
told me later that Pablito was indeed the perpetrator of the hate
letter; its watermark corresponded to that of his sketching paper.
He owned up readily enough when faced with the proof, and he
apologized profusely once he realized what a knowledgeable

guy his future brother-in-law was turning out to be.

The wedding ceremony went off smoothly. At the reception I was called on for a bilingual toast to the newlyweds. Prior to the cake-cutting, Glen was describing how on their return flight Vituca was able to pinpoint the aircraft's passengers by their accents. She would say, "Those people are from Buenos Aires," or, "That couple comes from Caracas," and so on.

This prompted someone to wonder, "What sort of accent does Mr. Trabler have?" to which Vituca (a soul of diplomacy, bless her!) quickly replied, "Mr. Trabler has *NO* accent--his Espanish is perfect!"

--o-**O**-o--

TRABLER BACKS PARTY-POOPERS

Although shameful and in retrospect difficult to condone, it nevertheless must be acknowledged that in the pioneer days of our nation success in "subduing the savage" was managed with barrels of booze. Unscrupulous traders introduced Indians and Eskimos to the white man's "firewater"as a means of obtaining better terms from the natives in their bartering transactions.

Occasionally, of course, this procedure would backfire when certain natives got too deeply into the alcohol and took to the warpath. The heads that planned the party then got scalped.

In the early days of the travel industry the big barons of big transportation similarly blandished their agents by bottle in an attempt to buy their loyalty. A railroad would launch a sales promotion, (and much later, airlines copied the same formula) by overwhelming their *protégés* with abundant libation.

My name is Terry Trabler. As owner/manager of a travel agency for more years than I care to remember, I vividly recall the days when such "presentations" took place.

The seminar site was usually a well-known hotel, although now and then it could be the posh Union Club or a trendy golf clubhouse or other recreation complex.

The program seldom varied. Drinks would be served to all and sundry along with hot and cold *hors d'oeuvres* or nibblies. After an hour or so, as the imbibing agents began to achieve a comfortable glow, the host sponsors would usher them into an adjoining room--where they were exposed to either a film or a slide show extolling the company's destinations and services.

"This drill is all fine and dandy,"said my friendly competitor Mike Johnson one night after such a seminar,"but your average Joe Blow agent reports to his office only a muddled version of what the promotion was all about."

"You mean a convivial atmosphere tends to impair cerebral retention?" I suggested, quoting from a recent trade magazine.

"Exactly, Terry. Speaking for myself, afer three or four drinks I'm apt to be a bit vague when it comes to recalling, say, an aircraft configuration or a categorical price structure."

"Good point, Mike. Which translates into relaying a half-baked picture to our clients, right?"

"Right on. We're actually failing them if we're not passing along a clear picture of what we supposedly learn at so-called professional sales presentations."

"So how can we improve on the situation?"

"Terry, I've been thinking about this for quite a while. If my people at Keating, you folks at Trabler, Gerry Smythe and his gang at the Auto Club and a few other top-producing agencies held a series of meetings, we just might come up with a dozen or two recommendations for suppliers. If enough of us got on the band wagon, they might even listen."

"You mean we'd go to the airlines, cruise lines, car rental agencies, tour operators and hotels, with suggestions on how they should run their business?"

"No, Terry. Only suggestions on how they could make their seminars a little more helpful and meaningful."

"Well, we can try. The idea's good, Mike, but most of these guys are quite hidebound and I'll wager we meet with sarcastic opposition--not necessarily from the reps themselves, but from the people in control."

"Terry, I always believe in giving the other fellow a chance to say his own 'no.' But if we keep hammering away, who can tell what we might achieve in the long run?"

- - - - -

The idea appealed to some of the other agents. It sounded so simple and logical. We would recommend that all suppliers' sales reps give out brochures to the agents at the *beginning* of each seminar. These would be gone over in depth, paragraph by paragraph, and price chart by price chart, giving everybody the opportunity to ask questions and take notes. Immediately after, when all the agents had absorbed the information, refreshments would be served as a reward for their patience.

Mike and I as spokesmen for the group, following numerous discussions and suggestions, outlined our deliberations to the various suppliers in our immediate area.

"You fellows must be out of your mind," they told us. "To begin with, by cutting out the customary liquor we'd probably draw less than half the normal crowd. And the no-shows would be circulating a garbled version of our message."

"But your message is garbled already," we protested. "In the current setup, by the time it gets to the agents most of them are too sloshed to sort out the details."

"Well, tough bananas, guys. We can't possibly undermine years of established tradition."

"But you're just working against your own interests since misinformation is worse than no information at all."

"Sorry. Even if you should be right, which we doubt, there is *no* way we could compromise. Our Higher-Ups call the shots and we're obliged to comply--no matter how you or we react. Orders are orders. Sorry, no deal."

After hearing the same line of reasoning from some twenty suppliers Mike and I felt as though we'd been tugged through a knothole backwards. What appeared to us a logical solution struck them as outrageous. Hell hath no fury like somebody whose pet addictions one tries to eliminate. Each call showed us what a tough job we'd undertaken.

"Don't propose doing away with a time-tested formula that everybody's happy with," one supplier quipped. "Upsetting a comfort station would raise a stink we'd never stifle."

So it continued, year after year. The same old rigmarole -- the same old diehard objections, even from people we took to be reasonably broadminded and innovative.

"Mike," I finally suggested, "instead of using this shotgun approach why don't we single out one particular supplier and really concentrate on getting his coöperation?"

"It might work,"he conceded. "So far we've tried just about everything else with no success."

"It would take only one adventurous soul," I pointed out, "to lead the way. Once the others see how the new procedure operates, and especially when they learn how much that supplier's business has increased through the experiment, they're bound to fall in line. The old domino effect, you know."

"Let's give it a try. Do you have a prospect in mind?"

"How about our biggest national airline?"

"I get it. The old prestige factor to sway the rest. It makes sense, Terry. The bigger they are, the harder they fall."

"Not exactly a nice thing to wish on an airline, but yes, I believe the psychology is sound. Let's get on with it, Mike."

"Already I'm cooking up some choice expressions to include in our pitch," he grinned. "This is going to be fun!"

Three evenings in a row we got together to polish up a hard-hitting argument to present to the airline people. Then we let it incubate over a weekend, in case something else should come to mind that we hadn't already considered.

Our reception at the airline was not exactly enthusiastic nor warmly welcoming.

"Here again, eh?" growled the District Sales Manager, "You guys never give up!"

"It's not a case of not giving up,"smiled Mike affably. "We just can't stand to see a knowledgeable DSM like you make an embarrassing mistake."

"My mistake was letting you in here once more," snorted the DSM. "I've already listened to your hare-brained proposal some umpteen times and each of those times I've explained why it wouldn't work. Okay, I'm giving you five minutes. But unless you come up with something brand new, out you go."

"Just in passing," I volunteered, "let us remind you that our two agencies, Keating and Trabler, are your star sales leaders in this area, as you yourself have admitted."

"I have no quarrel with that," replied the DSM.

"Well then," I continued, "in recognition of our dependable support, would you do us the favour of forwarding our recommendations to your head office?"

"In your covering letter," Mike chuckled, "you may call us any nasty names you wish, as long as you add that we are your star agents."

The DSM stared at us in disbelief. "You're asking me to bug my busy bosses with a daft idea they'll shoot down in flames? That could cost me my job. Or worse, it could trigger my transfer to some miserable little jerkwater place where Fat Alberts like DC-10s and 747s are still unknown."

"As Mike suggested," I remonstrated, "just lay any blame or indiscretion at *our* door, we don't mind. All we're asking is that you pass along our proposal and let *them* decide, okay?"

There was a long silence as the DSM thought it over. At last he looked up and grudgingly agreed. We couldn't get out of his office fast enough in case he'd change his mind. We'd finally made our point!

- - - - -

At the next airline sales seminar the agents were told that the evening's program would first consist of an appropriate briefing before gratifying their thirst. Brochures were distributed, queries were fielded, and, in a burst of well-being, the agents now felt they had stature and thrust.

Hardliners from the old guard, as predicted, decried such a flagrant departure from orthodox procedure. They belittled the serious "party-poopers" who sanctioned the "newfangled craze." Some went so far as to boycott supplier sessions altogether, and were abruptly taken to task with threats of losing their agency's appointment. For a while there was muttering or grumbling, but once the suppliers noticed the monthly increase in sales volume there was no looking back, and the agitators fell into line.

"In the long run, reason has won out," I remarked to Mike as we gratefully enjoyed some refreshment after a particularly fine seminar one evening. "It's a whole new ball game nowadays."

"For once," Mike agreed, "the minority voice has proved it quite plainly to dissenters that when we think before drink, our actions are a bit more responsible."

It didn't bother us at all that the airline District Sales Manager was now being hailed as a hero for having launched a new type of seminar (and not ending in a *miserable little jerkwater place where Fat Alberts were still unknown*).

--o-O-o--

TRABLER BOOKS A TRUCE CRUISE

"No *way!*" Her bangles jangled angrily as she pounded her fist on the corner of my desk. "If he plans to sleep with me the deal is off!" An obstinate lower lip emphasized her point.

"Now hold on, Letty," I argued. "I don't believe Hal wants to storm your guarded fortress as brazenly as all that. His only thought was for you to choose a comfortable stateroom, preferably on one of the upper decks, but not too far forward. And he made it quite clear that price was no problem."

"Well, he'd better not try any funny business. Because I just won't stand for it, see?" Again the obstinate lip.

My name is Terry Trabler. As owner/manager of a travel agency I sometimes get into delicate situations, particularly in dealing with clients who are also friends of long standing. Hal and Letty Brown were in that class. Married over thirty years with their children grown and gone, they'd recently separated and were now living apart. Hal, hoping to patch things up, had accepted my recommendation of a leisurely Caribbean cruise.

Hal Brown's thriving import/export business afforded him the privilege of occupying choice real estate in our city's most affluent area. He and Letty had been travel clients of mine for a decade and our families exchanged visits on a regular basis. Their children and ours had gone to the same school.

Hal was vague about the problems leading to his and Letty's separation except to indicate a misunderstanding so I let it go at that. I figured he'd probably elaborate some time later.

"Letty hatches some peculiar ideas at times," he told me in confidence, "but usually when I get home from the office I'm too exhausted to listen or to straighten out her thinking. Well, four weeks ago she suddenly packed her belongings and took off while I was at a trade fair. After a month of rattling around our big house alone, I'm fed up. The silence is unreal!"

"Some people would consider that a blessing," I suggested, but Hal's anxiety precluded appreciation of the humour of my remark. Accordingly, I tried another tack.

"Do you suppose Letty could be persuaded to join you on an ocean voyage?" I ventured. "Sort of a *truce cruise* in pleasant surroundings, to help you iron out your troubles."

Hal thought it over carefully. "You know," he mused, "that might be just the answer. Yeah. But the approach would have to come from you, Terry. Every time *I* try to phone her, she hangs up as soon as she hears my voice."

"That can be annoying," I agreed. "All right, as long as she doesn't hang up on me also, I'll diplomatically invite her into the office to look over some deck plans, so that she can make up her mind about a stateroom and a sailing date."

"Do you think you could talk her into a cabin with a double or queen-sized bed?" Hal wanted to know.

"That will depend on the ship and date she chooses," I told him, "and of course it will be subject to availability. Most of the vessels serving the Caribbean normally have twin-bedded cabins because of the climate. However," I promised, "I'll see what I can do." And that was how we left it.

So now, with Letty poring over deck plans and adamantly opposed to even token intimacy, I could see that some sort of compromise was in order. It would not be easy, but I had no wish to forfeit such a lucrative booking, particularly after the drop in sales volume our agency had lately experienced.

"Here's a nice large stateroom," Letty finally decided. "It's got two beds, good big cupboards and bathroom facilities, and a picture window rather than a porthole. Would you mind requesting that for us, Terry?" She consulted the deck plan again. "It's number **A-240** on the promenade deck."

"I'll check on its availability right away," I promised, "but if it should already be sold, what is your second choice?" I checked out the deck plan to ascertain that this particular ship offered absolutely no cabins with double or queen-size beds. Evidently Letty herself had also discovered this.

"Whatever else you can get on the same deck," she said, "as long as it has two beds and a picture window." She folded one of the cruise line's brochures into her handbag and departed.

I immediately phoned the ship's reservations office and was able to confirm the very cabin Letty had indicated. I called Hal with a progress report. "The liner Letty selected has only twin-bedded staterooms throughout," I told him truthfully, "but the accommodation is first-class, so I know you'll be happy with it. The cruise company needs a 25% deposit within ten days."

"I'll drop by and pay it this afternoon," Hal assured me. "I doubted she'd even go for the idea, so you must have done a good selling job. Anyhow, that's a step in the right direction. Thanks a lot, Terry. See you shortly."

Hal came over, happier than I'd seen him for quite awhile.
He paid the deposit -- said he was taking the rest of the afternoon off for a round of golf. He had barely left the premises
when the telephone rang.

"Travel with Trabler, good afternoon!" answered my secretary Cindy in her most engaging manner. "Yes, he's right here.
May I tell him who's calling?"

"It's for you, Terry. Mike Johnson from Keating Travel."

"Hi, Mike! Where can we book you today?" As one agent
to another, I naturally had to have my little joke. Except on
this occasion Mike didn't sound in a joking mood.

"Terry," he growled. "Did you reserve an outside double
on the Fantastic Cruise Line a little while ago?"

"As a matter of fact, yes, Mike, I did. Prime accommodation on the promenade deck. Why, what's the problem?"

"What's the problem, he says. I always give you people at
Trabler credit for running a clean business, but now I'm not
so sure. You just grabbed a stateroom that I've been trying
to get for weeks. They insisted to me that it was on deposit.
How do you guys manage to wangle space while the rest of
us go begging?"

"Now, just a doggone minute,"I countered. "I booked that
cabin myself in a routine manner. Nobody pulled any strings
as you seem to imply. Maybe it'd been cancelled just before
I phoned them, how should *I* know? Such things *can* occur.
Were you waitlisted for it?"

"Well, not exactly," he admitted. "As things turned out, I guess we should have been, though."

"By the way," I asked, "how did you infer that the booking was ours?" I knew that cruise lines are duty-bound to keep all such information confidential.

"It was only a shot in the dark," Mike said. "The fellow who wanted the cabin accidentally left behind a cruise line folder with No. **A-240** pencilled beside *your* agency's stamp on the back of the folder. Anyhow, I was able to get him a smaller cabin on the deck above. Sorry for chewing you out, Terry. Guess I blew my stack from frustration. Forgive me?"

"Only if you buy me a drink at the next travel seminar," I warned him facetiously. "Okay?"

"Fair enough. So long, Terry!" He hung up.

The troubled waters were calm once more, but on my way home after work I kept wondering whether that inadvertent dropping of our brochure in Mike's office could have been more than just a coïncidence. What if the fellow had got the pamphlet from Letty?

No one, other than she, had recently talked to us about Fantastic Cruise Lines, to the best of my knowledge. Now Terry boy, I cautioned myself, let's not imagine things -- you've been reading too many detective yarns, chum...

"Dinner is almost ready, dear," my wife announced as I got to our doorway, "and the Tuttles, you remember, are coming for bridge at eight-thirty."

"Yes, Doreen my queen, I do remember. Let's hope Fred will refrain from making any more unsubstantiated opening bids like he did last time he and Molly were here."

"Oh, Terry, that was just an accident—I'm sure he wouldn't have done it on purpose."

"Nevertheless, it completely ruined that hand for me. Right when I was counting on my first small slam of the evening."

Fred and Molly duly arrived and our card session eventually got under way. As Doreen was dealing, Fred remarked, "Sure wish I could deal cards as effortlessly as your wife, Terry."

He had told me this countless times before, but tonight I was determined to retain my good humour. "So, you've a problem, Fred?" I asked in a neighbourly way.

"It's these middle-aged arthritic fingers of mine," he went on to explain. "They don't react like they used to."

"According to Bob Hope," I quoted, "middle age is when you still believe you'll feel better in the morning."

"Oh, I *like* that!" Fred chuckled. "Hits the nail right on the head, doesn't it, Molly?"

Molly perked up. "Speaking of middle age," she ventured, "I saw your friend Letty Brown the other day, Doreen. She was having lunch at *The Snug* with--guess who? None other than that footloose old widower Pierre Breezy-Boy!"

"You mean *Brisebois*," corrected Doreen, pausing in dealing to allow this earth-shattering revelation to sink in."Well, well... Were you speaking with them?"

"Not really," admitted Molly in a disappointed tone. "They seemed too wrapped up in one another to observe a busybody like little old me."

"That's interesting," said Doreen. "There were rumours that she and Hal broke up because of some triangle thing. But we all faulted *Hal* rather than Letty."

"Well girls," I admonished, "let's get on with the game, shall we?" Doreen resumed her dealing, and I made a mental note of their comments for later consideration.

Next morning at my office, I received an early phone call from Hal. He sounded somewhat embarrassed.

"Terry, old man," he began, "do you think you might be able to, ah... reserve another cabin on that, ah... cruise sailing?"

"Have you then decided against the one Letty picked out?" I figured that maybe he'd had second thoughts about it, not due to the expense but because of the strained circumstances.

"Not at all,"Hal assured me, it's a dandy and we'll hang on to it. But you see--" I could sense his feeling for words. "I'd just like to order another cabin on the same ship. For a friend, you understand? It doesn't have to be on the same deck. In fact, it perhaps would be preferable in a different location entirely. If you follow my reasoning, that is."

"Actually Hal, you're a bit ahead of me but I'll try to catch up.

For booking purposes, what is this friend's name?"

"That's right, you *do* need a name. Well, Terry, couldn't you just put it under *mine*?"

"I'm afraid not, Hal. In international waters we've a passport situation, and stateroom passengers must be listed or they'll be denied boarding."

"You sure make it tough on a guy, Terry. Okay, I know you're just doing your job. Fine. I'll level with you; the name of the passenger would be Mimi Larochelle."

"The schoolteacher?" I was busy taking notes as we talked.

"The same. Now, don't think badly of me, Terry, although I know you're not the preaching type. It's just a sort of... well, *insurance*, if you like. In case I can't get Letty down off her high horse... well, the trip won't be entirely wasted, you see?"

"Yes, Hal."I tried to sound neutral. "Okay, it's your deal, but I'd advise playing your cards close to your chest. Just in case it becomes an explosive situation, old chap."

"So you'll get accommodation for her? Mum's the word, you understand, Terry. Life can be complicated at times."

"I'll phone you the moment the cruise line confirms a cabin. But it might take a while; the circuits are usually overloaded this early in the morning," I explained.

"Exactly. I'll await your call. And I repeat, mum's the word. Thanks, Terry."

Not only did I feel involved in a conspiracy, but I couldn't help wondering, with Letty's evident little scheme on the reverse side of the coin, how the whole situation would end.

I looked up to see Letty approaching my desk. She wore some sort of flowered creation, with matching wide-brimmed hat, and looked simply great. Her eyes sparkled. Also, she appeared to have forgotten her tantrum of the previous day.

"Morning, Terry,"she gushed. "I guess I'll need to complete a passport application for the cruise, won't I?"

"That's right," I nodded. "I'll get you one from the file."

"Could you please let me have two? Just in case I spoil it when I'm filling it out. It's always nice to have a spare."

Yeah, sure, I thought to myself. Spare application, spare spouse; what a rotten world we live in, really...

"Here they are, Letty. The address for the local passport office is on the envelope. They normally need three or four days to process it. Make sure your guarantor belongs to one of the categories listed. If you have questions, just call me."

"Thanks, Terry, you're a dear!" She sashayed out, and I got back to the phone to make Hal's other reservation. The lines were busy and I found myself on hold. A recorded message told me that my call was important and would be handled by the next available agent, provided I stayed on the line.

I turned around to find Fred and Molly Tuttle seating themselves beside my desk, as excited as two little kids.

"We saw an interesting ad in this morning's paper and thought we'd better check it with you," Fred announced. "It seems the Fantastic Cruise Lines are offering a big fare reduction on one of their Caribbean trips. Now, Molly and I have often spoken about taking a cruise. Here's a wonderful opportunity to try it."

He spread the newspaper out on my desk and--wouldn't you know it?--the date in reference was the sailing I had booked for Hal and Letty. I swallowed, trying hard to retain my composure. What the hell -- the more the merrier, and all the better for our monthly sales volume...

I got out the deck plan, explained the booking procedure to them, and let them make their first and second choice of cabins while I entered the necessary data in their file. After they had gone I resumed my time-consuming battle with the telephone.

By the end of the week I had everyone booked, passports in order and invoices issued for final payment. As the sailing date drew closer, I kept wondering how this hide-and-seek situation was going to end.

- - - - -

On the Monday, after the cruise was over, I had an ecstatic phone call from Hal.

"Letty and I are back together!" he exulted. "That shipboard scenario was exactly the tonic we needed!"

"Congratulations!" I said. "Tell me about it."

"Terry, you'll never believe it. In the ship's dining-room the first night out, the Chief Steward assigned us to the Purser's table, which seated eight passengers. At the same table he'd also put your bridge pals Fred and Molly Tuttle along with--oh, the irony of it-- Pierre Brisebois and Mimi Larochelle. And the eighth person was a Latin-American *Señorita* Chela Rodríguez, who obviously had a crush on the Purser."

"Quite a conglomeration,"I observed. "So of course, there was good clean fun for everyone."

"Well, things were, naturally, a bit sticky at the start. No one said a great deal. The general atmosphere was awkward and un-comfortable. But as soon as the wine was served and the Purser told a couple of funnies, everyone just relaxed and took part in the conversation. It got quite friendly and lively."

"Hal, don't keep me in suspense. You're going to tell me that by the end of two weeks, besides you and Letty resolving your differences, a mutual interest was developing on the Brisebois-Larochelle territory, right?"

"Right, Terry. But not in the way you think. You see, Pierre Brisebois took a shine to Molly Tuttle. Fred found wee Mimi to be the most fascinating creature since Gypsy Rose Lee."

"You mean the Tuttles have split up?"

"It would appear so. But give them time. When the euphoria of the cruise has worn off, things may look a bit different. In the words of my friend Terry Trabler, it was a *Truce Cruise*."

--o-O-o--

TRABLER FINDS CONSIDERATE CLIENTS

Many of today's consumers have short fuses. They are deman-
ding, impatient, and suspicious. Compared to a generation ago,
this chip-on-the-shoulder attitude is not the no-no but the norm.

In travel for example, a lot of clients will book on short notice,
frequently change plans, and cancel at the drop of a Stetson, with
never a hint of apology or excuse. It is miraculously refreshing,
then, for an agent to find a genuinely considerate client. Such
a person is the proverbial pearl-of-great-price, a giver of joy, and
an acquaintance to be cherished forever.

My name is Terry Trabler. In over 30 years of managing travel
agencies, I have learned to cope with the constant changes in our
industry and in the people who seek our service. So I cannot help
but reminisce on my dealings with two very special clients whom
I shall call Frank and Sally Oldster.

Frank and Sally were a senior couple who had farmed all their
lives. They had produced a family of four who now in turn were
raising families of their own, but keeping in regular contact with
their parents and siblings. Frank and Sally had long since moved
into the city and owned a neat and tidy bungalow just around the
corner from our main office. They had noted one of our window
exhibits featuring a forthcoming tour to South America, and had
dropped in for further information.

"Our son Jim is an engineer. He spent 12 years in Ecuador and
Peru with a petroleum company," explained Sally. "He used to
write such interesting letters about the people down there, and it
made us want to travel there some day."

"He shipped us a hand-tooled leather-topped coffee table for our fortieth anniversary," Frank said proudly. "So when we spotted your window ad on this next year's tour to that part of the world, we thought we'd come in and find out more."

"It's not too early for making a reservation, is it?" Sally asked anxiously, toying with the strap on her handbag.

"Not at all, Mrs. Oldster," I told her. "You do yourselves a big favour by booking well in advance. So many people wait until the last possible moment and are disappointed when they find a tour is sold out. And an exciting one like this fills up quickly."

"What all does it take in?" Frank wanted to know.

"First of all," I began, as I spread out a brochure in front of them, "we take a direct flight to Lima, rest up on arrival, and put in several days sightseeing the colonial aspects of the city, including many luxurious residences and public buildings."

"Jim mentioned a cathedral which displayed Pizarro's remains in a glass case," Sally confided. "Do we get to see that?"

"You certainly do," I smiled, "and next morning you have an early flight to Cuzco. I assume you're both healthy, because the altitude there is 11,500 feet."

"No problem," Frank assured me. "Sally and I are sound of wind and limb. There is no history of heart hurt in our family."

"Good," I said. "Your son Jim probably told you that Cuzco is the former capital of the Inca Empire. In its heyday that took in the greater part of South America."

"Yes, Jim mentioned that," bubbled Sally, "He said there's a three-hour train ride from Cuzco to Machu Picchu."

"Right, along the Urubamba River. Then, from the rail station, small buses take you up a steep winding road to the ruins of that Inca stronghold which the Spaniards never discovered."

I then described more of the tour: Pachacamac, Iquitos, the Yanamono jungle camp on the Amazon then Santiago, Bariloche and Buenos Aires. I got out our atlas and pointed to their next stop at Asunción. From there they would travel to Iguassu Falls, overnighting at the *Hotel DasCataratas* before flying to Brazil's Sao Paulo, where they would visit the Butantan serum institute and Ibirapuera park with its imposing Bandeirantes monument.

"When do we get to Rio de Janeiro?" asked Sally.

"On the Sunday morning before Shrove Tuesday," I replied. "That gives you lots of time to get caught up in the excitement of the huge *Carnaval* celebration and the Samba Parade."

"That'll be something even Jim didn't see!" exulted Frank. "He saw several smaller versions in Peru and Ecuador, but nothing like what we hope to witness in Rio."

"And don't forget,"I reminded them, "you'll also be able to visit Corcovado and take the cable car to the top of Sugarloaf Mountain for one of the most magnificent views in the world."

"Guess we'd better sign up while we're thinking about it, eh, Sally?"enthused Frank. "How much is the deposit, Mr.Trabler?"

We took care of the details: deposit, passport applications, health and cancellation insurance, arrangements for inoculations, and reading material to acquaint them with the contrasting areas of the tour. They left and I began reserving their booking.

As I had predicted, the tour attracted considerable attention and within a few weeks more than thirty people had signed up for it. Most of them were well-travelled. They had seen Europe, parts of Asia, "Down Under," and Africa, and were now reaching out for destinations that were sufficiently different to be desirable.

Frank and Sally gave me progress reports from time to time on how they were doing with their various preparatory exercises.We got the group together occasionally for audio-visual material and informal briefings on shopping and sightseeing. Each time we received new publicity sheets from South American countries we sent out copies to our participants. Everything was going so well that some disaster just had to occur to break the momentum and test our resourcefulness. And it did.

"Sorry to trouble you, Mr. Trabler," said Frank's voice on the phone, "but Sally has come down with a case of shingles."

"Oh, no!" I exclaimed. "I've heard that can be very painful."

"You're right. She's having a bad time of it. The doctor calls it *herpes zoster*. Says it stems from the same virus as chicken pox, which we both had as kids. She's broken out all over her right hip with clusters of tiny blisters."

"Is she in the hospital, Frank?"

"No, she's still home, and the doctor is treating her with daily shots of vitamin B-12. He also has given her some ointment to relieve the pain for the duration."

"How long does the doctor expect it to last?" Looking at the calendar, I noted that their departure date was still four months away. Then, thinking of Frank, I asked, "Is it contagious?"

"The doctor says it isn't and, depending on Sally's response to the medication, it could take anywhere from two weeks to a month to clear up. Do you think we had better cancel?"

"That would depend on Sally's progress," I said. "Let's give it a couple of weeks and see how she makes out."

"We both apologize for any trouble this may cause you, Mr. Trabler. It has come as quite a shock to us."

"Don't worry about inconvenience on *our* part," I told him. "Your top priority is getting Sally well and doing whatever you can to make things a little easier for her."

Shortly thereafter another couple actually did cancel, because of death in the family and the necessity of tending to executor duties connected with the estate. A young man who had booked as a single with the possibility of later finding a partner, was on the verge of changing his mind. New bookings continued to come in however. This was par for the course on a lengthy trip of the kind. We took it all in our stride.

When the Oldsters' two-week discretionary period had expired I had an excited phone call from Frank.

"Sally is almost completely recovered," he reported, "and her doctor says she should be able to travel with no difficulty. So I guess we'll hang in there. It would be a shame to miss the trip after all the preparations we've made, wouldn't it?"

"It certainly would, Frank. I'm so happy to hear that she's well again, and I know you'll enjoy the tour now even more."

"You bet we will. Oh, and thanks very much for the get-well cards from your office. Sally really appreciated them."

"You're welcome, Frank. After all, you two are part of our extended travel family and merit our collective concern."

The days went galloping by. Then, without warning, we had a phone call from Sally. She sounded somewhat aggravated.

"Mr. Trabler, when Frank went in for his regular medical check-up yesterday, the doctor discovered that the cataract in Frank's right eye is now overdue for surgery. On account of the shortage of facilities this time of year, he made an appointment for next Thursday, which he was able to do because the person scheduled for that date had just cancelled."

I looked at the calendar. The tour's departure date was now only five weeks away.

"What time period is involved?" I asked.

"The doctor says he'll have to be very careful for the first two weeks following surgery, so as not to risk infection. But, Mr. Trabler, his eye needs to adjust for six weeks before a revised optical prescription can be determined. That's a whole week after our tour will have begun. So we're really worried. Do you have any suggestions?"

"I believe we can work something out, Mrs. Oldster. Leave it with me for a day or so and I'll hope to have an answer."

I knew we had a directory of English-speaking physicians and surgeons in most parts of the world, and I needed time to cable for an appointment. Sure enough, I found an ophthalmologist listed in Santiago, Chile, and the tour would be stopping there for four days.

The time frame was exactly right. Frank would be able to get his new glasses in Santiago and use them on the remainder of the tour with no complications.

Sally was overjoyed when I broke the news to her.

"Oh, Mr. Trabler!" she breathed. "Frank will be so pleased when I tell him. Thank you, thank you! You've been so patient during our troubles. We must have been a real nuisance."

"Mrs. Oldster," I informed her truthfully, "if no one was more of a nuisance than you folks I would be fortunate indeed."

--o-**O**-o--

TRABLER FOLLOWS A DECENT FELLOW

Every so often, during the late fifties, Pete Shelby and I would lunch together. In Calgary, we both had gone to King George Elementary in Pleasant Heights, afterwards attending William Aberhart High School. Pete, due to his father's ill health, had to leave in mid Grade Twelve to help support his family, while I was fortunately able to enter University. I say fortunately, for I was no smarter than Pete, just luckier.

My name is Terry Trabler, owner of a chain of travel agencies. Although Pete used our services very seldom he was pleasant to deal with, and I always enjoyed his company. He was a decent sort of fellow with a dry sense of humour, despite misfortunes, both monetary and marital, which would have flattened a less optimistic chap. On one of our lunch dates however, he looked absolutely defeated. His eyes lacked their usual sparkle and his despondent manner, quite out of character with the Pete Shelby I knew, prompted my curiosity.

"Pete, old buddy," I said, "It's none of my business, but I never saw you looking so miserable. What gives?"

He laid down his menu and took a quick swallow from his glass before answering. He spoke slowly, in a low confidential voice while leaning towards where I was sitting.

"Terry," he said glumly, "How would you feel if somebody had saddled you with a support order of $400 a month for a child that wasn't yours?"

"You've got to be joking," I told him.

"No joke, Terry. I'm dead serious. And I've been tolerating this thing for three years now.What's more, I won't be finished with it until the kid is sixteen."

"But surely there must have been a mistake?"

"Of course it was a mistake. The entire set-up was based on purely circumstantial evidence. I happened to be on the scene at the wrong time. Wrong for me but absolutely great for some other people."

"Suppose you tell me about it."

Well, to summarize Pete's story, it seems that the poor guy had been bamboozled by a family of opportunists who knew an easy mark when they saw one.

Pete and his crew were doing renovations on a small grocery in the Kootenays owned by a Signor Giuseppe Rossi, who had moved there from the prairies in the Dirty Thirties. During the construction work Maria, one of Rossi's unmarried daughters, took a shine to Pete. She was "twenty-nine and counting," running to plumpness but still reasonably attractive.

Each work break would find her at Pete's side, teasing him in ambiguous small talk, or humming seductive operatic arias like *"Libiamo ne' lieti"* or *"Caro nome che il mio cor,"* while bringing him *cappuccino* and *biscotti*. This exclusive attention was not unnoticed by Pete's crew, who for ***their*** recess goodies had to dig into their lunch kits.

By the time the renovation was complete, Pete had become acquainted with all of the Rossi family--Papa Giuseppe, Mama Domenica, Maria's sister Luisa, and her brothers Marco, Luigi and Riccardo. On the final afternoon, the eldest brother Marco approached Pete, slapped him on the back and drew him aside for a hasty consultation.

"Look, *amico Pietro*," he ingratiated, "we have watched the masterful way that you and your men have tarted up our papa's store. You've done a great job and we're all impressed. Now today is my birthday, *è il mio compleanno*, so before heading to Calgary, why don't you come to the tavern with my brothers and me to celebrate? A fellow turns forty only once, and we'd sure love to have you join us."

Actually, Pete had planned to return home that same evening but being, as I mentioned, a decent sort of fellow, he thought to himself, "Why not? These people are eager to share their local scene with an outsider, and it would be boorish of me to refuse their hospitality."

So, after accepting Marco's invitation, Pete arranged to have his foreman and crew tidy up and take the van back to Calgary, saying he'd be on hand for their next job the following Monday morning. He also phoned the motel to reserve an extra night's accommodation, figuring that Marco and his brothers would undoubtedly celebrate until quite late.

He figured correctly. It was a Friday evening and the tavern was filled to capacity. Many of Marco's friends were aware of the occasion and insisted on toasting the birthday boy, waxing eloquent in the process and downing a considerable quantity of liquid refreshment. Poor Pete, unaccustomed to such copious amounts, found himself striving to keep up with the others. He also noticed that the room was beginning to sway a little.

Finally, politely but firmly, he apologetically left the roaring roisterers and staggered along to his motel.

"I'll just lie down for a short nap," he told himself, "and then I'll get up and grab a bite to eat." He noted the time, which was slightly past ten-thirty.

Moments later he was surprised to hear a knocking at his front door. Opening it, he saw Maria out there with a shopping-bag.

"May I come in?" she smirked. "My brothers didn't ask me to their celebration, so let's us two have a private one of our own, okay? *Conosco dei giuochi da adulti.*"

"Gosh, Maria," Pete started to say, but she pushed past him and shut the door behind her. In his befuddled state Pete was unaware of her not having locked it.

Maria took her shopping-bag to the coffee table and started to spread its contents out like a picnic display in a department store window. There was a bottle of Canadian Club, diet ginger ale for a mixer, and several cellophane sacks of various nibblies, presumably all from the family grocery.

"Now, if you'll be a *dolce tesoro* and get drinking glasses from the bathroom," she urged, "I'll get ice cubes from the dispenser and we'll have a nice little party, okay?"

"Just what I don't need at this particular moment," Pete told himself grimly. Still, as a decent sort of fellow, he decided it would be rude to send her packing. The glasses and ice appeared forthwith, and the command performance began to materialize. Pete, as one may surmise, was in no condition to put up an argument.

As a matter of fact, two more drinks reduced him to a state of confused babble. At this point, Maria insisted on disrobing him and putting him to bed. Shortly thereafter, she deftly removed her *reggisseno scollato* and *mutandine trasparenti* and joined him beneath the covers, still humming an operatic aria.

"Had you any perception of what was going on?" I asked Pete at this juncture of his narrative.

"Oh, I s'pose I was vaguely aware of it," he ruefully admitted, "but under the circumstances I was too crocked to worry about the consequences."

And consequences there certainly were. About midnight his door surreptitiously opened and in walked Marco and Riccardo on their way home from the tavern. Marco immediately left no doubt as to his interpretation of the cosy little scene.

"Just because we invited you to our party is no reason for you to tamper with our sister!" he barked. "*Now* we know why you were in a hurry to sneak out of the pub. A real *Don Giovanni* smart-ass, huh?"

"Now, look!" Pete was suddenly wide awake and deplorably sober. "It's not what you think at all."

"Oh, no? Caught making it in the sack and trying to say there's nothing going on. Well, we'll see about that, eh, Riccardo?" He grabbed Maria by the arm. "Maria, get on home before Papa discovers you're not in your room. We'll deal with Hot Pants here later."

The two brothers stormed out into the night. Maria hurriedly dressed, gathered up her shopping-bag items, and then staged an ostensibly recalcitrant retreat.

"Don't worry," she said before leaving, "I know how to handle those brothers of mine, and I'll see you tomorrow."

Pete, however, concluded that absence of body might surpass presence of mind. He wasted no time in packing his things and was out on the highway in half an hour. As we've said, he was a decent sort of fellow and detested arguments. Also, he knew nothing incriminating had taken place and he was in the clear.

Six months later Pete received a double-registered letter from the social services department which indicated a serious matter had come to their attention involving him and that he was to report to their premises immediately. Failure to do so, explained the letter, would result in immediate arrest by the police.

Pete was dumbfounded. "But this is ridiculous!" was his first reaction. "How can they lay charges against me -- when there's nothing to prove?"

He located the social services office, showed his letter to the receptionist, who ushered him into a tiny drab room containing a desk, three nondescript uncomfortable-looking chairs, and a bank of prewar filing cabinets lining one wall. Behind the desk sat a smug potato-shaped giant of a man, who motioned Pete to sit down, but omitted to introduce himself.

"Mr. --ah,-- Shelby," he began, "it is my unpleasant duty to inform you that a person called Maria Rossi has given birth to a baby daughter and has named you as the child's natural father. She requests financial support."

"But that's preposterous!" exclaimed Pete. "I never saw her in my life before this past summer."

"You wish to contest the claim?" frowned the social worker, rising from his chair to his full height of over six feet. "Court proceedings can be costly, you know."

"But how could the child possibly be mine, when I laid eyes on its mother for the first time only six months ago?" Pete had also risen to his feet, but felt intimidated by the other's greater bulk and obstreperous demeanour.

"My dear fellow, you must realize there is always a likelihood of premature birth, especially if circumstances have produced a disturbed condition."

"What if I demand a blood test?"

The social worker sat down and added a few more jottings to the notes he had started at the beginning of their conversation. He cleared his throat before replying.

"Mr. Shelby, blood tests for determining parentage can provide only marginal indications. Elements of an infant's blood not found in the mother's are inherited from the father. If the man lacks such components, he can in no way be the father. If, on the other hand, his blood sample *does* show those elements, it doesn't necessarily prove that he *is* the father, but merely that he *could* be. Proof of paternity would have to be established on other and more complicated grounds."

"So what are the man's chances?"

"About 50-50. But really, Mr. Shelby, this discussion is not getting us anyhere. Suppose you tell me your version of what happened and we'll take it from there."

So Pete resumed his seat and gave a pertinent recital of facts, interrupted randomly by the interviewer for clarification, as he took notes in a peculiar type of shorthand. At the end of Pete's story there was a long silence while the social worker reviewed what he had written. Finally, he spoke.

"Mr. Shelby, I wish to thank you for your unbiased and frank explanation of this unfortunate event. Also, I would like to point out that before contacting you our department ran an exhaustive check on your personal history in which we were pleased to note an absence of illegal activities, misdemeanours, and unsavoury associates. Your record is exemplary."

Pete waited for him to continue.

"Now, considering your unblemished background, it must be self-evident that litigation would irrevocably tarnish your reputation and credibility. Even one small indiscretion can ruin a man through an unkind media report. The critical public is quick to condemn. Do you follow me?"

Pete nodded in agreement. "So what do you suggest?"

"Merely that it would be in your best interest, brutal though it may seem, to gracefully go along with this woman's demands. If you tried to contest her claim it would soon become apparent that our family courts and laws are obviously a reflection of our basic social attitudes. An unwed mother publicly confessing her shame to obtain support for a helpless child becomes an object of great sympathy. The man named is traditionally a bounder and a cad."

"I still feel I'm being taken for a ride," Pete fumed.

"And it's quite understandable that you should. But a blasted reputation is a nasty alternative, don't you think? In any event, you can rest assured that for our part, these matters will be held in the strictest confidence."

So Pete reluctantly went along with the social worker's recommendation. It cost him $1,000 up front, followed by monthly payments of $400 each which, in the 1950s, was a fair sum.

"Well," I observed when Pete had finished his tale of woe and was sipping his coffee, "I don't blame you for striking out at the world in anger. It certainly appears that justice has miscarried. Why, it's nothing but downright blackmail."

"Blackmail it is, Terry, and it hasn't been easy. I've had a devil of a time meeting those payments, month after weary month, especially during the winter when my business volume has been at rock bottom. Believe me, many's the agonizing occasion when I felt like throttling that woman and her whole conniving family."

"They've really taken you to the cleaners," I agreed. "Tell me, Pete, have you any idea as to the real father?"

"How should I?" he growled. "For all I know, it could well be one of her evil-minded brothers. In any case the rotter obviously couldn't afford the aftermath, and that's how I got inveigled into being their ready-made scapegoat. But Terry, you haven't heard the latest dirty development."

"And what is that?"

"Some people are never satisfied. The woman has come to the conclusion that, since she found it so easy to share my earnings for the past three years, she must now increase her slice. She's asking $200 more a month. A sinking fund for the kid's future education."

"Good lord, Pete!"I exclaimed. "That's a whopping big jump. Fifty per cent, in fact. What do you intend to do about it?"

"I'm going to fight it, Terry. Damaged reputation or not, a guy can stand just so much."

We settled for our lunch and went our separate ways.

- - - - -

Several months passed before I heard again from Pete, a not unusual occurrence, since both of us were continually busy with one thing or another. He phoned me at my office one afternoon, and in his voice I sensed a suppressed feeling of excitement.

"If you've nothing better to do, Terry, how would you like to meet me after work at the Palliser pub? The drinks are on me."

"You've got yourself a deal," I told him. "About six, then, or or would six-thirty suit you better?"

"Make it six-thirty," he replied, and hung up, leaving me to wonder what new development had occurred.

Entering the Palliser pub at the appointed hour, I was happy to see that Pete had already arrived. He was strategically seated in a secluded corner. He caught my eye and motioned for me to join him. I instantly realized how relaxed he appeared, certainly happier and more carefree than he had been for ages.

"Glad to see you looking so fit," I remarked as I took the other chair at his table.

"Terry, if I felt any better I couldn't stand it," Pete grinned. "What'll you have?"

The barman came over and we placed our orders -- Pilsener for Pete and a Labatt's Blue for myself, nothing fancy.

"For a while this afternoon I thought I might arrive a bit late," I said. "One of my travel clients sauntered in only three minutes before closing-time. What gives, Pete?"

"Let's see. I guess the last time we lunched together I was in a bit of a bind. I must have been poor company."

"I won't risk your wrath by agreeing. But certainly, you had cause. I recall that your nemesis woman had upped the ante."

"Right. And I told you I was going to fight it, eh?"

"You did indeed, but I must admit I've seen nothing of it in the newspapers."

"I very much doubt that you will. Media nowadays are chasing after *sensational* items--a commonplace report about a disputed paternity claim would hardly qualify. But things got a bit rough there for a while, believe me."

"How did you make out?"

"I'm coming to that. One step at a time, okay? I phoned that social serpent and told him I absolutely refused to go along with the woman's demand for an additional $200 per month."

"What did he say to that?"

"What did he say? He threatened to have me thrown in jail, that's what. Which made me so angry I could spit. I hung up the phone, got in my car and fetched our family doctor and we hightailed it to that social service office with medical records to prove our point. They exonerated me in jig time."

Then came the revelation. Pete Shelby, a decent sort of fellow yet preposterously sensitive of certain shortcomings, reacted so violently to an accuser's greed that he grudgingly confessed a closely-guarded family secret. He was congenitally sterile.

--o-**O**-o--

TRABLER'S HOT-TO-TROT APPRENTICE

"We need to sell more package trips and cruises,"I urged my staff as we manoeuvred through our Monday morning meeting, "more groups, more charters, more special interest tours!"

We were trying to figure the reason for our agency's recent drop in sales volume. It was certainly not due to lack of effort by our employees. They regularly attended trade presentations and workshops, they kept current on the latest "in" destinations and the ever-increasing mess of special discounts and seat sales churned out by the airlines.

"Bread-and-butter bookings are important from a day-to-day standpoint," I conceded, "but they're not the crucial frosting on the cake. Unless we cultivate the big-buck business we're only order-takers, not top-producers."

"So please, Mr. Trabler, how do we go about it?"asked young Freddy Keen, our newest apprentice.

"Simply by concentrating more on the type of bookings that pay a better commission," I pointed out. "A cruise or package trip nets us, on an average, twice or three times what we earn from a bare-bones cut-rate airfare."

"And usually takes twice or three times less effort and preparation," chimed in Hank Granger, one of our senior travel agents. "All you have to do is find the right prospect and plant the idea. It's a breeze, really."

"And you don't have to spend the entire morning explaining a lot of crazy complicated airfares," offered Cindy, my secretary, who spent long hours on the phone doing just that when the rest of the staff would be out beating the bushes for new clients.

"But how does one find prospects for this big-buck business?" young Freddy wanted to know.

"First of all," I assured him, "you conscientiously have to learn all you can about each product. Get out to the seminars of the various suppliers. Ask questions. Keep up-to-date on changes that take place because, believe me, nowadays there are zillions of them."

"You can say that again," agreed Hank. "Nothing ever stands still in the travel industry. It's a daily dog-eat-dog proposition with every airline and tour operator out to make a fast buck."

"Which underlines my advice about knowing your product," I nodded. "When you have all the facts at your fingertips, people are impressed. You book them. If they like the way you have handled them, they'll tell their friends. Referrals from satisfied clients are what build up our sales volume. Never forget that."

"Oh, my!" exclaimed Cindy. "That reminds me. The Fantastic Cruise Line is doing a workshop at 7:30 this very evening at the Misadventure Inn. Their sales reps'll be phoning shortly for a nose count. Could I please have a show of hands?"

"Count me in!" volunteered young Freddy.

"And me!" from a half dozen of the others.

"Okay," said Cindy, taking a note of the number. "Now, be

sure you all go or they'll be on my neck tomorrow morning."

- - - - -

   Although I personally had gone to my fair share of seminars
and workshops over the years, I was now selective as to those
I attended, preferring to monitor reports from my staff. After
all, when a fellow is in administration, he has to set priorities
on demands for his time. In this instance, however, I decided
to put in an appearance at Fantastic Cruise Line's workshop
and learn what new trends might be developing. It's also nice
to swap ideas or opinions with one's competitors and catch up
on all the latest trade gossip.

   Accordingly at precisely 7:25 p.m. I sauntered up the steps of
the Misadventure Inn and headed for the main ballroom, where
a rumble of voices heralded the scene of the action.

   "Well, if it isn't old Terry Trabler himself!" The greeting was
accompanied by a hand on my shoulder, and I turned around to
recognize Mike Johnson from Keating Travel.

   "We don't see as much of you nowadays at trade shows, Terry
old chap. Are you slumming tonight, or is there something in
the wind that the rest of us haven't heard about?"

   "I have it on the best authority," I informed him in a phony
stage whisper, "that Fantastic are about to go bankrupt and are
offering their choicest staterooms at half-price."

   Mike entered quickly into the banter. "That news happens to
be a bit stale, Terry. The way I heard it is that they *already*
went belly-up. Their creditors are auctioning off their vessels

to the highest bidder!"

"Just goes to show," I said sweetly, "that the first liar never stands a chance. Come on, Mike, let's go and sample their free refreshments."

The ballroom was extravagantly decorated to represent the deck of a departing cruise ship, complete with streamers and balloons, make-believe passengers with gaudy paper hats and party noisemakers, a brass combo playing *"Anchor's Aweigh,"* and a general air of opulence and good-natured joviality.

"Now hear this!" announced one of the sales reps dressed in a captain's tropical uniform and speaking over the din through an electronic megaphone, "Passengers are requested to charge their glasses and proceed aft to our main lounge. Please hurry, for we have a special surprise awaiting you!"

"Do you think we're ready for any more surprises?" I asked Mike as we approached the "ship's bar" for our complimentary cocktail and other freebies.

"Let's be devils and find out, shall we?"

The aft lounge was already swarming with other travel agents by the time we reached it. A temporary stage had been set up and a cruise line employee was making introductory remarks.

"Sit back and relax folks, because you're in for a genuine treat. Fantastic Cruise Line takes great pleasure in presenting, direct from Mexico City's Fine Arts Palace, dancers and *mariachis* of the world-famous ***Ballet Folklórico!"***

As the curtain went up, a *mariachi* band broke into a lively version of *"Jarabe Tapatío."* Six couples in colorful costumes began a simultaneous performance of the vigorous hat dance. The audience cheered and applauded enthusiastically. After this first selection the program included several other regional dances, all executed with verve and professional flair.

Following the entertainment, of course, the cruise line reps went into their sales pitch. Agents, especially newcomers like Freddy, took copious notes and to their credit asked countless intelligent questions about the product.

- - - - -

Next day at the office, in the wake of an appreciative recap of the previous evening's workshop, I saw Freddy observing each office visitor in detail. He obviously looked for signs of the "big buck" category, and his eagerness was a refreshing contrast to the *blasé* attitude of the older staff.

A middle-aged couple entered, nicely dressed, and Freddy jumped forward to welcome them. One could sense that he sized them up as ideal cruising types and decided to pull out all the stops and make a spectacular sale.

"Good morning, folks!" he greeted. "Please be seated. My name is Freddy Keen." They shook hands. "And yours--?"

"Eugene and Peggy Jones."

"So nice to meet you. Perhaps, before we break out the brochures, Mr. Jones, you might like to tell us how long a period you plan to spend on your holiday."

"We are thinking of maybe a couple of weeks."

"Two weeks? And do you have a particular place in mind?"

"Possibly the Mexican Riviera."

"An excellent choice, really, and just the spot for you both to totally relax. It also happens that we have a two-week cruise that goes there, with lovely ports of call along the route. It's moderately priced and suits all ages. It permits a four-day stop in Acapulco to amply enjoy that fabulous resort."

"Well, honestly, we -- "

"'Scuse me, sir, one moment. We've got a folder here, giving you all the facts. Here are the category prices and a description of the optional shore arrangements. Best of all, with a cruise you have no sneaky airport tax. The beauty of a cruise, if I may say so, is this: once you're in your stateroom, you hang up all your clothing in roomy closets and leave them wrinkle-free, till you need them. You're not living from a suitcase as you would if you'd gone by air, and your meals are included in the ticket. No nasty hidden costs to catch you unaware."

"Young man, we really --"

"Pardon me, sir, I'd like to review with you the various ports of call. There's Mazatlán, Puerto Vallarta, Manzanillo, Ixtapa and Zihuatanejo on the way down to Acapulco, then Cabo San Lucas at the foot of the Baja peninsula on the way home, with an optional side trip to La Paz. You'll want to take lots of film for your camera, because each place is so picturesque. Believe me, you'll really have a ball!"

At this, the Joneses jumped up from their chairs and turned

around to head back out the door.

"Young man, your pushiness is unacceptable. We attempteed to interrupt, to tell you that cruising is the last thing we'd have wanted -- each of us spent twenty years in the navy!"

TRABLER INVESTIGATES INDIA

"One of my suitcases is missing," Mrs. McQuaddy told me. We were transferring our baggage from the train to several waiting taxicabs, before checking into Clarks' Shiraz hotel at Agra, site of the famous Taj Mahal.

"Are you sure?" I asked. "How can you tell?"

"Well," she grumbled, "I watched one of the porters load up my first bag on top of two others he was balancing on his head. The other two belonged to somebody else. He dumped all three into one of the cabs and went back to the train cart for another load. But the three he picked up then were other people's bags."

"Now, hold on a moment, Mrs. McQuaddy. There are more porters than *that* one handling our baggage--have you watched what the other fellows unloaded as well?"

"Of course I did," she sniffed. "And my second suitcase is a bright paddy green. I would certainly have spotted it in spite of all this hubbub and confusion, if it were being put into a cab."

"Fine, Mrs. McQuaddy. After they finish transferring them we'll do a bag count and compare it with our manifest."

Terry Trabler is my name and selling travel is my game. I've been "telling 'em where to go" for three decades, and I must be doing something right, for the majority come back and rebook.

We were nearing the end of a month's de luxe tour of India. It had been arranged through that country's government tourist agency's Canadian office at substantially reduced rates in a bid to attract new business for a developing destination. The year was 1972, and the ongoing unpleasant confrontations between India and Pakistan had not escalated to their current volume.

We flew by Air France from Montreal to Paris, and by Air India to Bombay, checking into the posh Intercontinental Taj Mahal hotel near the Gate of India dock. Next morning some launches took us ten kilometres across the Bombay harbour to the small island of Gharapuri, home of the famed Elephanta Caves. On arrival, we had a choice of proceeding to the caves on foot or being carried in a sedan chair for a couple of rupees.

We oohed and aahed at the underground sculptures carved in the hollowed-out sandstone over a long period, dating back to the eighth century and dedicated to the god Shiva and his consort Parvati, shown in colossal relief.

Following four days' sightseeing and shopping in and around Bombay, we were flown to Bangalore. Our hotel there was the Ashoka (named for an early emperor) which had quite a scenic entrance driveway and a lovely swimming pool. In Bangalore we visited their 18th century Lal Bagh botanical gardens with a big collection of rare tropical plants. The city's domed Civic Edifice reminded some of us of British Columbia's legislative building in Victoria. Not surprising, for the latter's architect Francis Rattenbury in his boyhood had been familiar with colonial India's structural design.

Early next morning, carefully driving on the left side of the highway -- a carry-over from the era of British rule -- we made our way to Mysore, 138 kilometres distant, passing many an oxcart and divers ditchdiggers. We stopped halfway, at a group of shops specializing in handicrafts and ingenious toys, reasonably priced and extremely well made.

"Did you notice those hills on the horizon?" asked Kenneth Kitching, a tour member from New Westminster. "They almost appear to take on the shapes of India's better-known animals."

"Now that you mention it," said Mrs. Daphne Dalrymple from Calgary, "that middle one looks to me like a crouching lion."

"And the bulky one beside it could certainly be taken for the head of an elephant," opined Mitch Morley of Revelstoke.

These three had stepped down from the tour bus and were seated around a roadside outdoor café table, slaking their thirst with glasses of fresh mango juice. Others snacked on roasted cashew nuts, which in India take the place of North America's ubiquitous salted peanuts.

Daphne Dalrymple lowered her voice and hunkered down, assuming a posture of serious confidentiality.

"I really wonder about that Mrs. McQuaddy," she murmured. No one seems to have a good word for her, and she retaliates by flaunting a nasty chip on her shoulder."

"She does appear to be somewhat of a loner," admitted Mitch. "But then, what else would you expect of someone who has spent her whole life in a little jerkwater town like Jaffray?"

"Jaffray. Where exactly is *that*, by the way?" asked Ken.

"About halfway between Cranbrook and Fernie, just off the

Crowsnest Highway and the Kootenay River. About 25 kilo-metres from the trout hatchery at Wardner," explained Mitch. "What you'd call a one-horse town -- if you were sore at the horse!"

"Still, the place must have *some* redeeming feature," ventured Daphne, "even though it obviously isn't Mrs. McQuaddy."

"From the moment we left Montreal," observed Ken, "that woman has never stopped complaining. First it was her seat on the plane. Said she felt hemmed in. Then she found fault with the way her meal was served. At our Bombay hotel she didn't like the idea of having a phone in her bathroom. Insisted it was an invasion of her privacy."

"And did you hear the way she chewed out poor Mr. Trabler when she thought she was overcharged for the sedan chair to the caves?" commented Daphne. "Actually for a woman of her size and weight, I would say those four struggling porters were considerably *under*paid."

"I'll tell you *one* thing,"said Mitch, "I don't wish to be judged antisocial or dissatisfied with our journey up to now, but I did book this tour for enjoyment. And that testy Mrs. McQuaddy doesn't exactly fit the picture."

"Let's get back aboard the bus," I advised the group. "We are still only halfway to Mysore!" I couldn't help overhearing the last of the McQuaddy conversation, and I wished I hadn't. It is the duty of a tour escort to establish and maintain a reasonable aura of compatibility within his group, even though one or two of its members take a fiendish delight in being non-conformist. The prime ingredient for harmony is a good sense of humour.

In Mysore we admired the elegantly constructed temples and buildings, the Maharajah's palace (now converted to a hotel) and the exquisite parks and monuments.

"See the huge statue of Mahisha the demon-killer?" chuckled Ken. "I guess that's India's equivalent of Paul Bunyan."

"Except that this guy is missing a blue ox," said Mitch. "Do you recall the sculpture in Bemidji, Minnesota that time?"

"I do indeed. I snapped a photo of it. The name of the blue ox was Babe, of all things."

"Yeah. According to the legend, it measured 42 axe handles and a plug of chewing tobacco between its horns."

"I guess such tall tales originate because the lumberjacks are constantly surrounded by tall trees."

And speaking of tall trees, our next stop was Cochin, which boasted more lofty coconut palms than any place we had been. We soon found that the locals had capitalized on this situation, for there was an enormous factory making doormats from the coconut shell fibre. Cochin's local tour guide provided us with a detailed demonstration of each phase of the operation, including the weaving and carving of designs and names in the more expensive mats. He also drew our attention to another interesting bit of anthropology.

"These factory workers are all senior citizens," he announced, and yet none of them has grey hair. Can anybody tell me why?"

His question met with a deafening silence.

"Their hair has not changed colour," he proclaimed, "because all their life they have never eaten red meat. Just fish."

"Now that I've found *that* out,"snapped Mrs. McQuaddy, "it's too late to do *me* any good. I'm a senior *already.*"

This time her complaint produced amused laughter.

Boarding a breeze-conditioned launch, we slowly circled the island, pausing for a look at the age-old immense Chinese fishing nets being lowered into the deep by levered poles made of shaved coconut palm tree trunks. This picturesque but entirely practical method had been passed on from generation to generation for centuries.

After visiting the ancient Portuguese church of St. Francis, where at one time the remains of explorer Vasco da Gama had been buried, we lunched at our seaside Malabar Hotel.

At 2:00 p.m. we boarded a plane and headed to Trivandrum and Kovalam Beach, at the southernmost tip of India where, on a clear day, one could nearly see across the Gulf of Mannar to Sri Lanka.

We overnighted at the Kovalam Palace Hotel and enjoyed a morning tour of Trivandrum's museums, art galleries, zoo and aquarium. Late in the afternoon we were again airborne, this time for Madras, on the tropical Bay of Bengal.

In Madras we bedded down in the elegant Connemara Hotel. We were all encouraged to put our shoes outside the doors of our respective rooms each night, to find them nicely polished the next morning.

"I should have packed a few more pairs," pouted the seldom satisfied Mrs. McQuaddy to no one in particular. "I certainly don't get that kind of service back in Jaffray."

Sixty kilometres south of Madras we had a tour of the coast village of Mahabalipuram and its fine examples of Dravidian monolithic art that flourished from 600 to 750 A.D. Elephants, camels and lions were expertly sculpted from single pieces of solid granite, and so well preserved that they appeared to have been done within the last decade.

A bit farther south we were welcomed to Silversands, a neat, serene beach resort with thatched cottages which, despite their primitive exterior look, were all fitted inside with truly modern luxurious facilities.

"I've never seen such a lovely beach," vowed Ken Kitching, "and that includes our favourite summer spot at White Rock. But why is it so deserted?"

"Good question," said Mitch. "I was wondering that myself."

"Maybe it's something to do with the sea water," conjectured Daphne. "I guess the Indian folk perform their daily ablutions in rivers, like the Ganges. Possibly from religious beliefs."

"Last one in is a piker!" shouted Mrs. McQuaddy, dashing out from a cottage in an outmoded swimsuit which she practically overflowed.

"C'mon, you guys -- this is too good to miss!"

Several other tour members had also changed into swimwear

and were heading for the breakers.

"What about sharks?" wondered Daphne.

"Mrs. McQuaddy is home free," pontificated Ken, "since the local guide swears Bengal Bay has only *man*-eating sharks!"

"Not exactly a tasteful joke," Mitch observed. "One of those predators may just forget about male bonding and find the lady in question a tempting morsel."

"Did you say *morsel*?"asked Daphne. "Now *that* definitely is what I would call a gross understatement."

"It's all relative, Daphne," said Ken. "Compared to the size of those sea monsters, McQuaddy is merely a mouthful."

"Please, *please*, ladies and gentlemen," interrupted their bus driver. "Sorry, but no time for swim. Bus must leave in fifteen minutes for return to Madras!"

"Wouldn't you know?" sighed Ken. "Just when we might have seen a ready-made solution to the McQuaddy dilemma, it gets blocked by our native bus driver's penchant for punctuality."

"Never mind, Ken," consoled Mitch."Trip's not even half over yet. Still plenty of time to get back on track. Opportunity can present itself in many other ways."

So, to the dire dismay of the would-be surf soakers, the bus driver rounded everyone up, loaded us on his vehicle and took us back to Madras. Two days later we flew to Delhi, where we checked into the luxurious Ashoka Hotel. Once again Mrs. Mc-

Quaddy got to beef about the phone in her biffy. Our windows overlooked Nehru Park, with the Hotel Akhbar in the distance.

Next morning we drove out to the Qutab Minar, a victory tower built about 1200 A.D. by Sultan Qutab-ud-Din, founder of Delhi's so-called slave dynasty. Then we visited the nearby famed Iron Pillar, made of pure malleable iron in the fourth century A.D. When one leans backward against it and reaches both arms around the circumference, one is assured of a prosperous future if one's right and left fingertips touch together on the other side.

"Poor Mrs. McQuaddy," observed Daphne. "Despite much squeezing and grunting, she didn't quite make the grade."

"I noticed that," agreed Ken. "It almost broke her heart."

"But not to the same extent as when she had to miss out on her swim in the Bay of Bengal," said Mitch. "This was mere superstition while the other was sabotage by the bus driver. I suppose we could term it a delayed denouement."

Our tour included the Raj Ghat, commemorating the place where Mahatma Gandhi's body was cremated. Then we took in the Gandhi Memorial Museum, theRed Fort, Pearl Mosque, Jama Masjid, and the circular Lok Sabha parliament building. We also stopped at an ivory mart, where we were invited, one and all, to purchase our fill of precious knick-knacks.

Finally, the morning arrived when we boarded the train for a three-hour journey to Agra and the Taj Mahal. It was right at the Agra railway station that Mrs. McQuaddy was certain her paddy-green suitcase had gone missing.

"I know for sure they didn't put it in one of the taxicabs," she reiterated, "because it's such a bright green colour. I certainly couldn't have missed seeing them handle it, Mr. Trabler."

"All right, Mrs. McQuaddy. Just as soon as they finish loading we'll do a bag count and check it against our manifest."

"These guys are too slap-happy,"she decided."They joke and laugh so much, they're not paying attention."

In spite of Mrs. McQuaddy's insistence, however, the count agreed with the total number of pieces originally loaded on the train in Delhi. Her acceptance of this piece of information was anything but gracious.

"If that bag doesn't show up I'm suing somebody," she swore at least three times under her breath.

Our first sight of the Taj Mahal was intensely dramatic. There it stood in quiet splendour, so strikingly perfect in form that all other structures seemed clumsy by comparison. Over 20,000 labourers, masons, stonecutters and jewellers took 20 years to build this mausoleum, which emperor Shah Jahan considered worthy of the love his empress had borne him in their 19 years of married life.

Our leisurely morning tour of the edifice was only a preface to what followed. We viewed Agra's Red Fort -- compared to Delhi's, it was a blend of both Hindu and Muslim architectural styles. We saw the imposing tomb of Itimad-ud-Daulah, once prime minister of the state. Other sightseeing ensued, but the crowning experience was the re-visiting of the Taj by the light of a full moon that same evening.

As we strolled around the building, the white marble reflected the moonbeams in a sort of ethereal translucence, emphasized by the sparkle of thousands of gemstones encrusted in its walls. It was not just something to see, but the unique experience of a lifetime. Had we seen nothing else, our journey would have been worthwhile.

Returning to our hotel, I was accosted by the desk clerk who handed me a telegram. From the bell captain of the Ashoka in Delhi, it read as follows: "REQUEST PERMISSION FOR DISPOSAL AND/OR FORWARDING OF GREEN SUITCASE FOUND LEFT IN ROOM RECENTLY OCCUPIED BY MRS McQUADDY STOP KINDLY REPLY UPON RECEIPT."

"This will take some diplomacy," I said to myself.

--o-O-o--

TRABLER MEETS THE MILLENNIUM

"Don't be a dope!" I shouted to Mel. "It's too dangerous, I tell you, and you won't get a second chance!"

He made an impatient gesture of defiance.

"Listen, Terry," he argued, "if I *don't* go in there we'll never really know for sure, now, will we?"

I frowned my exasperation and appealed to his logic. "But if you *fail* to come back out -- we *still* won't know," I countered. "Look, Mel, if you insist on doing this I refuse to be responsible. Because whatever happens to you in there won't be *my* fault and that's *that*."

- - - - -

Looking back on those tumultuous times from the safe vantage point of this year 2025 I smile in recollection, though even now I get caught up in the excitement as I think about what occurred, what did *not* occur, and what *could have* occurred if only things had worked out differently. Back then we were more cocksure, more foolhardy and, let's face it, twenty-five years younger.

My name is Terry Trabler. I have managed travel agencies for more years than I care to remember. Like anyone in business, I have had good years and bad years. Most of my office activity has been routine, even boring. But every now and then someone or something comes along to pose a real challenge and just such a something punctuated my first meeting with Mel Manicky.

The moment he entered our building I found myself thinking, "This guy isn't the usual run-of-the-jet client by several hundred airborne kilometres."

To begin with Mel Manicky wore a jump-suit. Yes, a genuine, down-to-earth dirty, rumpled, sweat-stained jump-suit, yet peeking out beneath the legs of his slacks were two highly-polished, immaculate patent leather ballroom shoes. To further add to the incongruity, an old greasy-looking navy blue beret surmounted his practically hairless head. Humorously incredible, (as I told myself at the time) yet apparently straightforward and harmless.

"How may I help you?" I asked as he unceremoniously seated himself opposite my desk before being invited to do so.

He laboriously extracted a crumpled newspaper clipping from an inside pocket and pushed it across to me over the desk.

"Saw your ad in this morning's *Gazette,* so thought I'd drop by for a bit more detail,"he explained."The name of your tour truly whetted my interest. It's so...well, uncharacteristic compared to the usual type of travel offering. Shows originality."

"Well, thank you," I said, glancing down at the paper he had proffered. Perhaps the guy was not so eccentric after all, for I privately considered this particular blurb to be a good example as to how all travel advertisements should be worded--no deceptive or ambiguous gobbledygook, just plain honest facts.

"MEET THE MILLENNIUM IN THE MARITIMES!" it said, and went on to describe a 20-day winter tour of New Brunswick, Prince Edward Island, Nova Scotia and Newfoundland, culminating with a New Year's Eve party in St. John's.

The lucky party goers would be the first in Canada to welcome in the year 2001, since the rest of the country would celebrate the occasion from a half to five-and-a-half hours later. The vast spread of time zones from coast to coast, including a half-hour differential between Newfoundland and the remaining Atlantic provinces, created this anomaly.

It was Trabler Travel's own unique concept and, to date, no other agency had mimicked our idea. Owing to the time of year, many seasonal tourist attractions were unavailable. Still, by stressing our excellent standing with leading tour operators, we wangled a few concessions.

These were a sleigh ride through New Brunswick's 391-metre Hartland covered bridge over the Saint John River, and another taking in Kings Landing Historical Settlement at Prince William, a visit to CFB Gagetown downriver from Oromocto, and a spectacular view of the Bay of Fundy tidal bore.

Our tour members would also enjoy crossing to Prince Edward Island via the new 13-kilometre Confederation Bridge, besides landmarks like the Green Gables home, Charlottetown's Confederation Centre, Halifax's Citadel and Old Town Clock, Peggy's Cove, and the St. Francis Xavier University at Antigonish.

Weather permitting, they would also negotiate Cape Breton's scenic Cabot Trail, with a stop at Baddeck to see the Alexander Graham Bell Museum, and later to relish a ceremoniously orchestrated lobster feast with top-to-toe apron-size napkins to catch stray splashes.

"May I ask a stupid question?" ventured my colourful visitor, after digesting the foregoing recital of attractions.

"No question is necessarily stupid," I disarmingly smiled, "as long as it fits the subject being dealt with."

"Right on,"he admitted. "That answer qualifies you as a pro in your field. Well, sir, I'm no pro. Just a dabbler who tries to live one day at a time without hurting anybody."

"That can apply to most of us," I said. "So now, let's hear your impending question."

"Simply this," he explained. "Your ad shows the actual ground portion of the tour commencing at Montreal and returning home from St.John's. I assume that the air fare between here and both places is included in the price of the overall tour?"

"That's correct," I assured him. "Actually, all such information can be found in our tour brochure. Here is one, by the way."

"Thanks."He rapidly scanned the folder."I think I'll sign up for it right now. How much of a deposit do you need?"

"Ten per cent of the tour cost," I told him as I began to fill out a new file form. "Excuse me, may I please have your name?"

"Melvin Manicky," he grinned."M-A-N-I-C-K-Y. Rhymes with *panicky*, although I assure you there's no real connection!"

I got his address, phone number and other statistical data, wrote a receipt for his deposit, and acquainted him with several useful details that had come to our attention following the printing of our brochures. He departed happily, with no explanation for the beret, jump-suit, or ballroom shoes. His attitude just seemed to imply that anyone in their right mind would do business in such attire as a matter of course.

A week or two later we had a visit from Clancy Coddler, the local branch manager of Timely Tours Limited, with which we had set up and coördinated our "millennium jaunt" through the Maritimes. Timely Tours was a vibrant Canada-wide operation which had grown rapidly in recent years because of its imaginative approach and thorough, painstaking attention to detail.

Timely specialized in organizing a kind of tour just different enough to appeal to the well-travelled segment of our clientèle who looked for more than mere repetitions of previous journeys. The *"been there and done that"* set was constantly on the alert for new ideas, and Timely created the titillating ticket it sought.

"Thought I'd pop in to congratulate you on how well you folks are doing on that New Year's effort,"smiled Clancy. "Considering there are still a few months to go before it gets under way."

"Thanks, Clancy. Our advertising did the trick, eh?"

"Oh, the ads helped, Terry. But the folks you've been signing up are anything but the usual rag-tag-and-bobtail."

"Impressive names, eh, Clancy?"

"Well, I should say. The list you've sent in so far looks a bit like the local *Who's Who.* Men like his worship Mayor Glenn Gladly, symphony *maestro* Mario Menomosso, chief of police Benjamin Bookem, all with their respective wives..."

"And don't forget our G.P. Dr. Stephen Stethoscope and the town's corporation lawyer Lucifer Loophole," I interrupted. "I can anticipate some lively dinner conversation during the trip!"

"Right, Terry, right. But what I'm wanting to know is how you managed to hook a famous guy like Mel Manicky, huh? I'll bet *that* took some fast talking on somebody's part."

It was *my* turn to be stopped in my tracks.

"Hang on there, Clancy," I said. "Just what do you know about this fellow Manicky? Who exactly is he?"

Clancy's jaw dropped in genuine surprise.

"You mean you don't know him? C'mon, Terry, surely you read the newspapers now and then."

"I have to admit I've been a little too busy lately for either the papers or television," I said. "What with paperwork, attending travel seminars, opening a new branch, I've probably missed out on a lot of things. So bring me up to date, eh?"

"Okay, Terry. For your belated information, last month Melvin Manicky won the lottery jackpot. Seven-and-a-half million. He has been quoted by reporters as saying he has invested the entire amount and won't be frittering it away on frivolous fancies."

"You don't say!" I remarked as matter-of-factly as I could.

"I find it hard to believe," observed Clancy, "that you've been absolutely ignorant about this. Why, it's been the chief topic of town gossip for three weeks now."

"Guess it just passed me by. Anyhow, he'll be an interesting addition to our Maritimes tour group, don't you think?"

"That's quite an understatement, Terry. I'm almost tempted to join the jaunt myself. I suppose you and Doreen'll be escorting it to keep it running smoothly?"

"We hope to. But it's a family time of year and we haven't yet got everything sorted out. I'll let you know in plenty of time."

"Do that. Well, Terry, I'll run along now and take care of my other calls. Keep up the good work!" He whistled his way out.

- - - - -

"Doreen, honey," I said to my wife at dinner that evening, "it seems I've been so busy with work-related items that I've been out of touch with the world at large. Had my head buried in the sand, like an ostrich. But quite innocently, of course."

"Yes, dear," she acknowledged. "I noticed your preoccupation, but figured you'd snap out of it in time. You always have."

"Tell me," I went on, "what you know of a chap by the name of Melvin Manicky."

"Manicky? Why, he's the fellow who won the big lottery last month. The papers were full of it for days. Many of the local gals have been practically mobbing him."

"Because of his sudden wealth?"

"Naturally. But as a young single bachelor, he has also now become ver-r-r-y eligible!"

"That figures. What else did the papers have to say?"

"Well, they did mention some of his hobbies. He goes in for ballroom dancing I know, and he recently qualified as a private aircraft pilot. Also, I believe he collects bats."

"Baseball bats?"

"No, no. The flying kind that inhabit belfries and caves."

"You don't say... Still, I suppose that would be a bit more exciting than chasing after butterflies. Does he stuff them?"

"The papers didn't say. But, Terry dear, why are you all of a sudden interested in the doings of this man Manicky?"

"Because, Doreen my queen, this man Manicky as you call him came into our office a week ago, and signed up for that special *Millennium in the Maritimes* tour."

"Oh my. How will he get along with people like Mayor Gladly, Ben Bookem, and Lucifer Loophole?"

"You're right, dear. It promises to be an intriguing mix of personalities. I'm rather tempted to forego the Yuletide season at home this year and escort that very tour. Would you like to accompany us and share the fun?"

"Well-l-l, we've always had a family Christmas before, but I guess the others could get along without us for just this once."

"Okay, my love, I'll make the necessary arrangements. And I'll leave it up to you to find a peaceful solution as far as the rest of the family is concerned."

"You're all heart, Terry. It won't be easy, you know."

"I suppose you're right," I admitted. "At any rate, dear, I do appreciate the info on Manicky. What you've told me explains his fondness for berets, jump-suits and dancing shoes."

- - - - -

December was on us before we realized it. The weather was unseasonably mild, and we looked forward to an enjoyable trip. Melvin Manicky had specified single occupancy hotel accommodation, as had two or three others of both genders, but the majority of us were in either twin or double rooms throughout.

For Mayor Glenn Gladly's benefit I had written and e-mailed mayors of other cities we planned to visit, and all had assured him and us a royal welcome. Maestro Mario Menomosso had reserved seats for some of us at symphony concerts in Fredericton and Halifax, and chief of police Benjamin Bookem arranged to escort a select few on a tour of New Brunswick's Dorchester Penitentiary.

At the Baddeck Museum in Cape Breton, Dr. Stethoscope intended studying Alexander Graham Bell's "vacuum jacket" invention which preceded the iron lung. Lucifer Loophole wanted to pore over the Confederation document in Charlottetown.

Clancy Coddler and his wife Molly joined us, and all told we had a manageable congenial group of 36 people. Mel Manicky had earlier confided to me some exotic plans for exploring the caves at Rocks Provincial Park by the Petitcodiac River mouth at Hopewell Cape, New Brunswick. Since this area was not on the route laid out for us by Timely Tours, he arranged through his home flying club to rent a twin-engine Cessna 402 in Fredericton and, accompanied by myself as map-reading navigator, he would fly there during the tour's free time in the provincial capital.

According to the guide book, the park's fame stemmed from its topheavy formations of soft rock resembling grotesque overgrown flowerpots. These reddish pillars, capped by balsam fir and dwarf black spruce, had been shaped by centuries of frost, wind, and ferocious tides surging up the Bay of Fundy.

At high tide the towering "flowerpots" -- up to 15 metres in height -- became small islands. At low tide, park visitors could descend stairways, walk along the shore and explore the caves and cliff crevices. A warning whistle would sound when the tide was coming in.

"Actually," Mel assured me, "I've carefully checked the tide tables for that date. There'll be plenty of time for me to make my explorations and get back up to the waterfront restaurant. We'll have lunch there, or maybe a quick coffee, and then we can fly back to Fredericton before dark."

"Sounds great," I said. "Let's hope for good weather."

During the months since our first meeting I had got to know Melvin Manicky rather well. He'd succeeded in handing me a revised interpretation of his hobbies and ambitions.

"The media don't always portray a person in the best way," he told me. "They normally latch on to some out-of-the-ordinary custom or characteristic that they hope will attract attention to their assessment of someone."

"And in your case?" I asked.

"Well, to begin with, they had me collecting bats. I don't *collect* bats -- I merely study their flight patterns."

"So how do you go about it?"

"I film their various movements with my camcorder. There are over 500 species of flittermice -- as I prefer to call them -- most of them subsisting on insects and fruit."

"What about vampire bats?"

"Vampire bats are not nearly such deadly creatures as many people imagine. They don't *kill* people, but, like mosquitoes, leeches and other unpleasant wildlife, they *do* suck the blood of fowls and domestic animals when they get a chance, which they seldom do."

"I once read about a man who fell asleep on a beach and one of those vampire bats punctured a toe with its sharp teeth, and siphoned off quite a bit of blood before he woke up."

"Oh, it does occasionally happen, but they don't often get a chance like that. Mostly they feed on fruits and insects. At any rate, to get back to what I started to tell you, I have so far recorded flight patterns of more than a hundred different species of them, including red ones, little brown ones, silver-haired ones, Sri Lanka flying foxes, flower-nosed ones from the Solomon Islands, and Indian plantain bats with orange-coloured bodies."

"But, Mel, what is your purpose in all this?"

"My purpose? Terry, I'll let you in on a little secret. When I was in high school we studied a very interesting account of the many invention intentions of Leonardo da Vinci. As you know, most of his ideas were centuries ahead of their time."

"Yes, indeed. In more ways than one."

"Well then, one of his ideas was for a human-operated flying machine. But he based his diagrams and designs on the actions of **birds**. To my way of thinking, a much more relevant system should emulate the flight of *flittermice.* We human beings are in no way built like birds. Our structure favours four-footed mammals."

"By golly, Mel, that's a very logical conjecture."

"So much so that I'm surprised no one seems to have thought of it in all those years up to now.   I can't imagine how anyone with half a brain could have missed it."

"And just exactly what have you in mind in connection with your intended exploration of the Rocks Provincial Park in New Brunswick?"

"As you know, Terry, bats customarily migrate to a warmer climate in winter. But at Hopewell Cape, a colony of English pipistrelle bats inhabits one of the caves year-round -- owing to an unusually mild climate in that area.   Pipistrelles are a lively species.   They fly swiftly and make all sorts of sudden turns or quick dives in search of insects for their subsistence. This final filming will wrap up the first phase of my project."

Tour departure day arrived, cheery and bright, with the usual eager sense of excited expectation, even for practiced old hands such as Doreen and myself. Most of our passengers were at the airport in good time for the customary formalities, the facetious farewells to relatives and friends, as well as joking predictions of our baggage and ourselves ending up at the same destination.

Mel Manicky took a bit longer than the rest of us to clear the security checkpoint, due to his voluminous photographic items, but shortly thereafter we were all in the holding pen, impatient for the flight attendant's signal at departure time.

In Montreal the next morning, following a restful night at the Queen Elizabeth Hotel, we boarded our bus for the Maritimes. Clancy Coddler, microphone in hand, jostled a position next to the driver and began a factual -- and frequently fanciful -- commentary on various noteworthy landmarks along the way.

On arriving at Fredericton, Mel was hungry for action. "As soon as we check into our hotel," he muttered to me, "let's get out to the commercial air field and take off for Hopewell Cape. We have to make the most of every minute before that blasted tide comes in from the Bay of Fundy."

I had prepared Doreen for my absence on Mel's bat jaunt, so she'd arranged for a shopping spree with the other wives at the Regent Street Mall, then a visit to the famous Beaverbrook Art Gallery to contemplate paintings by Reynolds, Gainsborough, Constable, Hogarth, Winston Churchill and Salvador Dalí.

"And you two be very careful,"she warned. Many times wives (bless them!) can anticipate things long before the rest of us. I often wonder how they tolerate us "lesser mortal" husbands.

Perhaps more by good luck than good management, my map-reading abilities got us to the Rocks Provincial Park in jig time, and Mel landed the Cessna in a nearby field after getting clearance from local authorities via the aircraft's transponder. We unloaded all the video gear and headed for the stairway leading down to the huge "flowerpot" rocks and their adjacent caves.

Mel wasted no time selecting the cave he wished to explore.

"How do you know which cavern houses the bat colony?" I asked in all seriousness.

"It's quite simple, Terry. All you have to do is look for the cave mouth marked by their droppings. See?" He pointed to the evidence as he spoke, evidence I'd thoughtlessly ignored.

"Now," he continued, "from here I'm on my own. I'm used to handling what has to be done next, and if more than one person enters the cave it creates needless confusion. The flittermice, if suddenly awakened by unfamiliar sounds or voices, can react with considerable violence."

"I understand," I said. "So you go ahead and do your thing, and I'll kill time looking around until you return."

He disappeared into the cave, gingerly tiptoeing while doing his best not to rattle any of the equipment he carried. An hour went by. Two hours. Three. Suddenly I heard an ear-splitting blast from a steam whistle in the area, and realized it was the incoming tide warning we had read about in the guide book.

Sure enough, there was the Bay of Fundy surf approaching at an alarming pace. Where was Mel? Hadn't he heard the whistle?

Just as I had almost given up on him, he emerged from the cave mouth in a leisurely offhand manner and ambled towards me.

"Got some dandy shots," he grinned. Then, in practically the same breath, he let out a howl of desperation.

"Holy mackerel!" he shouted. "I've left behind two cartridges I just finished taking. Here, Terry." He handed me the gear and took off. "I'll be right back."

"You can't go there now!" I hollered. "The tide's nearly here. We've got to run for it!" But he was already out of hearing and sight, back with his flashlight into that confounded cave.

Meanwhile, the salt chuck was sloshing over my shoes.

- - - - -

I'll never know just how we got out of that predicament, but somehow or other we made it with seconds to spare. The pumping of our adrenaline must have alerted our guardian angel, for that was the closest I've ever come to definite disaster. As we reached the stairway top and looked down on the seething mass of swirling sea below, the full significance of what could have happened hit us with a sickening thud. We didn't even stop at the restaurant for coffee, although we most certainly needed it.

The rest of the journey proceeded as planned. We reached St. John's in Newfoundland sufficiently early to welcome the new millennium before the rest of Canada. Everyone declared that our excursion had been a splendid success. Mayor Gladly, Chief Bookem, Maestro Menomosso, Dr.Stethoscope and legal Loophole all managed to accomplish their pet objectives.

Doreen and the other wives did their art gallery tour and shopping spree. Mel Manicky started work on his bat-plane project immediately after returning home.

Someday during the next twenty-five years I must tell Doreen how she nearly became a young widow.

--o-**O**-o--

TRABLER TACKLES TRAFFICKERS

The office telephone rang.

"Travel with Trabler, good morning!" answered my secretary Cindy in her merry-Monday-even-if-it-kills-me voice."Yes, he's right here... may I tell him who's calling?"

"For you, Terry. Hugh Leessom from Rent-a-Rover Thrifty Car Hire Corporation." She spat out the words like cherry pits.

"Morning, Hughie--how are the rentals running these days?"

"Not up to expectations, Terry. That's why I'm phoning. Do you recall a client of yours by the name of Skip Towner?"

"Sounds familiar. Hang on for a moment, Hughie, while I check the files... Yes, here he is: two-week hotel and car rental package, to visit trade shows in three cities. Bought health and accident insurance as well. New client, referred to us by John Pringle at Frantic Airlines, from whom he had booked flights. So, how can we help you?"

"Terry, he was supposed to have returned the car to us last Friday. We had reserved that vehicle for a weekend client and, when it didn't come in, we tried to phone Towner but got a recorded message that his number was no longer in service. On Saturday one of our staff drove over to the address he'd given, which turned out to be a vacant house -- boarded up and abandoned, in fact."

"Son-of-a-gun!"

"Exactly. So we're in a bit of a bind, Terry, and needing your assistance. Do you happen to have any other information on the guy? Who else might he have dealt with?"

"Hughie, it runs through my mind that he mentioned previously having booked through Mike Johnson at Keating Travel. So just sit tight, while I check with Mike and Frantic Airlines, okay?"

"Fine. Please get back to me as soon as you possibly can. I don't fancy bothering the police until it's absolutely necessary, because once *they're* in the picture it could drag on forever."

"I understand," I told him. "I'll do my best to call you back within the hour."

"Thanks, Terry; I knew you'd help." He hung up.

After several attempts to reach the airline and getting only a busy signal, I phoned Mike Johnson at Keating Travel.

"Mike, what can you tell me about a former client of yours named Skip Towner?" I asked when he came on the line. There were a few moments of silence, then an explosive interjection.

"Don't touch him with a ten-foot pole!" Mike advised with vehemence. "He's a deadbeat and recently took us for a bundle."

"Thanks, Mike, but evidently it's already too late." I told him the circumstances and asked whether he had any ideas as to what we might do to catch up with the guy.

"We've already exhausted the possibilities," Mike said. "He's as slippery as a slice of liver. He keeps moving from place to place. He's obviously discovered that it's cheaper to move than pay rent. So far though, from what you tell me, he hasn't taken the trouble to change his name. With his record there must be a pretty strong reason for retaining it."

"Probably an insurance angle," I surmised. "Mike, can you re-call some hobby or pastime this rascal indulges in? Any sort of new lead might give us a fresh follow-up. And that would be to your advantage as well as ours, you know."

"Hm-m-m... Come to think of it, Terry, I believe the guy's a bit of a pool shark, since on one occasion he dropped into our office with a cue case over his shoulder. Also, he probably attends har-ness races, for he once accidentally left a dope sheet behind on coming in to pick up an airline ticket."

"Okay," I said. "For the moment we'll forget the racing angle. But there are five pool halls in town. Between our two offices, we've enough people to cover them during slack periods, on the off chance of spotting Towner and following him to wherever he's moved in the meantime."

"Yeah. The idea's good, Terry, but what if he suspects he's being followed? An ugly customer like him could be dangerous, as you well know."

"Not if our guy is cautious and unobtrusive, Mike. He doesn't have to make a meal out of his intentions."

"All right, then, let's give it a try. But if we run into trouble, don't say I didn't warn you." He hung up and left me to contem-plate this last happy little thought.

I phoned Hughie Leessom at Rent-a-Rover and filled him in on our plans. Hughie was ecstatic.

"Hey, that's great!" he exulted. "We'll give you a hand if you like, because the more people we have out there the better our luck should be in bringing the scoundrel to heel."

Somehow I felt a bit apprehensive but it's pretty hard not to be swayed by such enthusiasm, especially after Mike's reluctance.

"Fine, Hughie. The more the merrier, but just make certain your fellows understand what might occur if their quarry wises up and reacts with violence."

"No problem, Terry. I'll spell it out to them so there'll be no possibility of anything going wrong."

Driving home from work later, I found myself inadvertently perceiving a spot newscast on the car radio. "A scam involving rental vehicles has recently come to light," the announcer said.

"It appears that well-organized groups are hiring cars, quite often on stolen credit cards, then dismantling them and trafficking the parts to legitimate service shops or junk dealers. Police and car rental agencies ask the public to notify them of suspicious transactions that may come to their attention."

Oh sure, I reasoned. What profiteer in his right mind would be likely to divulge the source of his revenue? However, that newscast disturbed me. What if the car taken by Towner had already fallen prey to traffickers? He'd had it for two weeks. There'd be nothing to prevent his doing it and all his continual moving could hold him virtually trace-proof. Although Hughie had not hinted at it, I wondered now whether prior knowledge of the scam had prompted his original call to me.

I also wondered just how Towner had managed to put one over on Mike Johnson at Keating Travel. I rated Mike as one of the most competent agents in the city and not easily hornswoggled. This guy Towner, then, whom I recalled only vaguely, must be a convincing character. In fact he had played me for a sucker as well, so we were up against a scofflaw who would fight like a wolverine to keep ahead of the game.

Next morning I called Hank Granger and Freddy Keen into my office. Hank was one of our senior consultants. Freddy, as an apprentice, was still learning the travel business.

"Fellows," I began, "we've got ourselves a problem that's just a bit different." I told them about Skip Towner as well as about the newscast concerning the spare parts traffickers.

"Hank, your house is within a block of Pete's Pool Parlour. There's only an off-chance of that car still being in circulation until now, but here's a description of it just in case, complete with serial number. Freddy, you're a frisbee throw away from Blackie's Billiards so here's *your* copy of the car's description. Keep your eyes and ears open, both of you, and phone me the moment something breaks, okay?"

"Mr. Trabler, may I ask a question?"

"Go ahead, Freddy."

"Suppose we should spot this Towner fellow. Isn't he likely to recognize us from seeing us in the office?"

"Good point, Freddy. However, since he dealt directly with me at the counter so close to the entrance I doubt that he would remember either of you even if he *did* notice you in your dark little back corner. Any other questions?"

"Does his sport pattern include *curling*?" asked Hank. "With a nickname like Skip, this could be a distinct possibility."

"It could indeed, Hank. Fine. If you feel like checking out curling rinks as well, so be it. But don't spend so much energy on the case that you neglect your clients. Business comes first."

Freddy and Hank had scarcely left when Cindy informed me that Hugh Leessom was on the phone.

"What developments, Hughie?"

"Terry, you'll never believe it. One of our salesmen spotted Towner getting into that same Rover by Blackie's Billiards."

"Son-of-a-gun! Did he follow him?"

"He started to, but the guy zoomed out of there as though he'd been sent for, and our man lost the trail soon after."

"Oh, tough bananas! So after all the excitement we're back to square one, eh?"

"Wait, there's more. About an hour later another salesman noticed the Rover parked beside Vic's Curling Arena, which is just around the corner from our office here. He phoned me. I sped over in the tow truck and quickly and quietly removed our violated vehicle before Towner even knew what happened."

"It probably would have spoiled his game," I smirked. "Set-backs like that can put a chap off his customary stride. So what was your next move, Hughie?"

"We found a document with his address in the glove compart-ment and passed it on to the police. They arrested him and he'll appear in court tomorrow."

"Good going, Hughie. I'll inform Mike Johnson and we can all take it from there."

"Oh, Terry!" came Hughie's muffled voice as I was about to hang up. I put the receiver back to my ear.

"I owe you at least a drink," he promised me.

--o-**O**-o--

TRABLER TESTS TRADE UNIONS

"The tiny Costa Rican has challenged the hefty Nigerian to a duel," they told me excitedly, "and he's so determined, we can't talk him out of it. See what you can do."

I glanced outside, where a small group huddled ominously by the administration building. I recognized Peruvian delegates Fausto Flores and Fernando Tarazona, together with Mexicans Iñigo Damián and Enrique Camarena. Also visible were Pedro Pinto from Chile, Ninan Alexander from Singapore, Oscar Rodríguez from Cuba, and Timothy Ogum from Ghana.

All of them, in grim bewilderment, were trying to fathom a terse monosyllabic argument between undersized, pink-faced Jorge Espinoza and massive tar-black Mike Labinjo whose big purple caftan billowed in the mountain breeze like a spinnaker of a racing yacht, making him look even larger. It reminded one of a cocker spaniel nipping at the heels of an elephant. Neither adversary apparently understood each other's language.

"It is a question of honour, *señor*," explained Espinoza to me in Spanish when I reached them. "He has insulted not only myself but my homeland as well, and I demand satisfaction!"

- - - - -

My name is Terry Trabler. As manager of a travel agency, I had arranged transportation for scores of foreign delegates to a two-week seminar at the Banff School of Fine Arts, scheduled for September of 1957. Sponsored by the International Confederation of Free Trade Unions with headquarters in Brussels, the seminar logistics had been worked out by the Canadian Labour Congress, the ICFTU affiliate in Canada.

Due to my fluency in French and Spanish, two of the seminar's official languages, they invited me to join their crew of regular on-site translators. This, in addition to travel arrangements.

Specially-chosen key unionists from North, South and Central America, Europe, Asia and Africa were lodged in the Fine Arts chalet facilities for the two-week period, along with a staff of translators, interpreters, stenos and typists.

With the huge assembly hall arranged for plenary sessions, stand-up placards on the long tables proclaimed the name, land, and labour affiliation of each registered delegate. A battery of tape-recorders linked a public address system with a circuit of headphones for simultaneous interpretation *à la* United Nations. Three walls were banked with multilingual study aids.

The first task for us translators, none of whom had served an apprenticeship in Tin Pan Alley, was to write a Spanish version of the unionists' hymn *"Solidarity."* Sung to the tune of *Battle Hymn of the Republic*, it involved the following lyrics:

> *"When the Union's inspiration through the workers' blood shall run*
> *there can be no power greater anywhere beneath the sun;*
> *for what force on earth is weaker than the feeble strength of one?*
> *The Union makes us strong.*
> ***CHORUS:***
> *Solidarity forever, solidarity forever, solidarity forever;*
> *the Union makes us strong."*

After a half-hour's cogitation and discussion we came up with the following, which was appreciatively endorsed by numerous Hispanic delegates:

> *"Cuando inspira sangre obrera la idea de la Unión*
> *no hay poder mayor en dondequiera se levanta el sol,*
> *porque no hay fuerza alguna donde no se ve fusión.*
> *Nos fortalece la Unión.*
> ***CORO:***
> *Solidaridad siempre, solidaridad siempre, solidaridad siempre;*
> *nos fortalece la Unión."*

An election by regions created a ten-man student council, and lectures during the seminar were supplemented by daily multilingual bulletins, summaries, press releases, and impromptu bull sessions during break periods.

The atmosphere was charged with a sense of urgency. Determination by each delegate to capture and retain every vestige of information contrasted refreshingly with the casual attitude of many current-day school students.

- - - - -

To return to their duel scene, I tactfully ascertained that big, good-natured Mike Labinjo had jocularly greeted the Latin delegate in English as a "Costa Rican son-of-a-bitch." Fiercely patriotic Espinoza had misconstrued the non-intentional epithet as a slur on his nation. According to Labinjo, Nigerians customarily used the phrase as a harmless term of affection, paralleling, one supposes, the equally innocuous British north country habit of addressing relatives and close friends as "ye buggah."

After a brief bilingual clarification, I managed a conciliatory handshake between the involved parties and Mike's unfortunate *faux pas* was promptly accorded the insignificance it deserved.

Misunderstandings of the sort were, happily, a rare departure from the harmony that usually prevailed. The delegates' fervent dedication to the job at hand applied equally to their social activities. During the two-week seminar, national independence days were celebrated by Costa Rica, El Salvador, Guatemala, and Mexico. The entire student body and staff participated in each of these festive occasions, with profoundly emotional overtones. Exotic beverages were produced by the said countries and ceremoniously consumed. One such event held a moment's silence for all the world's workers who had fallen in combat.

Costa Rica's contribution was particularly noteworthy. Puny Jorge Espinoza, aided by his compatriot Rafael Sancho, tossed back his head and burst into their country's national anthem:

"¡Noble Patria! tu hermosa bandera expresión de tu vida nos da; bajo el límpido azul de su cielo blanca y pura descansa la paz."

All present were astounded at the force of Espinoza's rendition, and one listener found it remarkable that such a powerful voice could come from such a small body.

"No problem," boomed big Mike Labinjo. "Canaries, sparrows and frogs are typical examples." Luckily Espinoza either missed this observation or failed to understand it and so averted another grave international incident.

In fact, Jorge at the time was attempting to explain through an interpreter that Costa Rica's anthem had been composed in 1852 by Manuel María Gutiérrez, a military bandsman, when merely

23 years of age, and that its lilting lyrics were the inspiration of poet politician José María Zeledón.

The inevitable lighter side surfaced also. In the dining room one evening, someone suggested that each delegate say a few words of wisdom in his own native language. One by one they gladly complied. Each dissertation, though meaningless to the majority, nevertheless received enthusiastic applause.

The most eloquent in his remarks was Chandra Dixit from Lucknow, India. Listening with rapt attention to his impetuous delivery, we instinctively felt that here was drama, brilliance, and power... his performance impact produced a prolonged and tumultuous ovation. We later discovered to our collective mortification that what he actually said meant, "I used to believe that all fools were in India. Now I know otherwise!"

Translation difficulties sometimes arose with the necessity of putting into terse Spanish literary gems like "An empty stomach does not dwell on high principles" which we eventually worked into *"En estómago vacío no cabe nobleza de alma."*

American and Canadian delegates were highly amused by the reaction of participants from tropical countries to the first light snowfall in the mountains, which occurred halfway through the seminar. Grown men, who never in their lives had seen snow at close range, delightedly felt it, tasted it, rolled in it, threw it at each other and even took samples to their rooms with appropriately embarrassing results.

Pint-sized Jorge Espinoza appeared to have an affinity for getting into difficulties. On his way to the dining-room one day for breakfast, he surprised an enormous black bear at an upturned garbage can just outside the kitchen. This, Jorge decided, was a photo opportunity too marvellous to miss. So he quickly turned and scrambled back towards the chalet for his camera. The big bear, attracted by sudden movement, and evidently sensing it to have been activated by fear, took after him in hot pursuit. The garbage could wait -- here was live meat! Completely oblivious to the fact that the intended victim was scrawny and probably had not dined since the previous evening, the big black bear instinctively felt the spirit of the chase and was rapidly closing in.

- - - - -

Mike Labinjo was enjoying breakfast with friends from Ghana, Jamaica, Barbados, and Malaya. All of them were hearty eaters and greatly appreciated the extravagant portions served by the dining-room staff. The staff, delighted that their efforts met with genuine satisfaction, plied their charges with generous helpings. These people didn't pick at their food, they decided, and it was fun to appease such appetites and hear such lively conversation.

"Our plantation people are strongly unionized," explained Noël Emmanuel from Malaya, "and their wages are greatly improved in comparison to the old days. Their children are getting better grades in school and going on to higher education."

"That goes for our transport staff at Ebute-Metta," said Mike Labinjo. "Especially those in administration. Their kids have ever so many more opportunities than *we* did."

"In Jamaica our biggest problem is keeping the youngsters in school," reported Wes Wainwright. "There is so much tourist traffic and easy money that they shortsightedly live only for the moment." He paused and glanced out the dining-room window.

"Good heavens!" he shouted. "Look over there--a huge bear!"

All eyes turned in the direction of his pointing and stared in disbelief. Labinjo yelled, "That's the little Costa Rican guy it's chasing. C'mon, fellas, we'd better hurry!"

Nearly overturning the table in their rush, they dashed out through the door, shouting in an effort to frighten the animal. It ignored them and continued after Espinoza, who by now was almost at the door of his chalet.

The bear finally reached her two cubs beside the chalet. No one had noticed them before. Their mother, apparently imagining them to be in danger while she foraged for their food, now rejoined them and all three disappeared into the forest.

Espinoza missed getting his photo and his would-be rescuers heaved a deep sigh of relief. "Lucky son-of-a-bitch!" exclaimed Labinjo. This time there were no repercussions.

--o-O-o--

TRABLER TILTS WITH TAILORS

In a lifetime of travel, my transactions with tailors in various lands have been amusing, enlightening, embarrassing, frustrating, and quite frequently incredible.

Hong Kong, for example, prides itself on the ability of its tailors to manufacture quality garments more cheaply and more quickly than elsewhere. My first encounter with one of these hotly competitive clothes factories was in 1970 while escorting a tour group to Expo70 at Osaka, Japan. Our itinerary included five shopping and sightseeing days in Hong Kong, which gave us plenty of time to sample the available merchandise.

Our group occupied a posh hotel at Kowloon's ocean terminal where some 125 ships come and go daily. Around the corner from Nathan Road's huge neon signs, wall-to-wall pedestrians and double-decker buses, my wife and I saw an establishment called *Peninsula Men's & Ladies' Outfitters Ltd*. Intrigued by its name and appearance, we decided to check it out.

"Good morning, distinguished guests!" a smiling attendant greeted as we entered. "Welcome to our Peninsula. Please be so good as to follow me." He led us to a spacious inner salon that easily could have served as a fashionable family parlour. Its tasteful furniture included comfortable sofa and armchairs, coffee tables, and ornate chinaware cabinets.

"Please be seated," our host invited. "My name is Victor Wu. Would you care for tea, coffee, or perhaps something a little stronger, while you relax and enjoy inspecting our assortment of materials?"

"Thank you; a cup of tea would be very nice,"my wife Doreen replied. I chose a Scotch and water. Mr. Wu excused himself and quickly reappeared, first with our beverages, and soon after with several swatch books, which he obsequiously spread out beside our drinks on the coffee table.

"Please take your time," he cajoled. "There is no hurry. Does Madame wish more hot water for her tea?"

"Perhaps a little later, thank you," said Doreen, giving her attention to all the samples. "Such lovely materials, Terry. It's going to be hard to decide, don't you think?"

Personally, I had no problem picking out a couple of attractive serges for winter wear, and a China silk for summer. Women as a rule appear to need more time to reach their decisions, but eventually Doreen had settled on two exotic cocktail dresses, a *cheongsam*, two evening gowns and a lady's business suit. Our measurements were taken with infinite care by two different tailors, and we were asked to come back Thursday for a fitting.

Following a day of sightseeing at Victoria Peak, the Tiger Balm Gardens, the resettlement area, Repulse Bay, Deep Water Bay and the teeming fishing village of Aberdeen, we boarded a *sampan* to dine at the Sea Palace Floating Restaurant where we chose our seafood from a huge tank of live crustaceans and got a bit more practice in the art of using chopsticks.

Next day we went by hydrofoil to the Portuguese harbour town of Macau, at the mouth of the Pearl River, 40 miles from Hong Kong. We watched while one of our fellow tourists won thirty Hong Kong dollars, playing blackjack at the posh Lisboa hotel casino under a large ornate chandelier.

Doreen and I had our scheduled fitting at the Peninsula Men's and Ladies' Outfitters, again accompanied by the beverage of our choice, in separate rooms now because of the "gender gap."

I'd barely undergone the chalk-marking drill and was leisurely enjoying my Scotch when Doreen rejoined me with a bottled-up air of amusement on her expressive face.

"What gives?" I asked, noting that she was just bursting to relate an apparently humorous incident.

"Well," she confided, "the chap who fitted me for the lady's business suit was the tallest Chinese gentleman I've ever seen. He had a really deep voice, although he hardly said 'Boo!' all the time he was finding what alterations were needed.

"Suddenly, right after he'd chalk-marked around my shoulders and neck, he strode ahead to the front, backed up a few paces, then muttered something sounding suspiciously like Chinese."

"Could you by any chance repeat it?"

"He said, *'One high, one low.'*"

"Meaning?"

"Well, you see, dear, we left the hotel in such a mad hurry this morning I didn't realize, until the man's remark, that I'd improperly adjusted my bra!"

- - - - -

Also befitting the *"Sorry I Asked"* department is an episode I

experienced in London, while on an autumn tour of the British
Isles. Having a free afternoon, I had gone to a smart Chelsea
shop for a nice ***macho*** suit of Harris tweed, several days before
we were scheduled to set out for the Scottish Highlands. At that
happy phase of my life I boasted what is known to the trade as
a "poor man's figure," signifying that, nine times out of ten, I'd
be able to wear a suit right off the rack with no alterations.

In this particular instance, however, probably because of high
carbohydrate indulgence during the tour, my measurements did
indicate that several adjustments were called for. As the fitting
proceeded I noted the tailor making frequent notes on his work
sheet in a sort of abbreviated shorthand. In certain areas he had
entered cryptical observations like *"Na.Wst." "Sh.Rch.," "Sl.St,"*
and *"P.S."*

"Pardon my curiosity," I remarked, "but if it's not betraying
any esoteric trade secrets could you possibly enlighten me as to
your notations on the measurement sheet? For example, I'd pre-
sume that *'Na.Wst'* meant 'narrow waist,' right?"

"Very good, sir. That is absolutely correct."

"And the others?"

"If you would excuse me, sir, they are rather personal. One
could p'raps be offended, sir. Does one really have to know?"

"You're dealing with one who is reasonably thick-skinned," I
assured him. "I come from a large family and am not likely to
be provoked. Certainly, go ahead -- ***this*** one can take it."

"With respect, then, sir, *'Sh.Rch'* signifies 'short reach' and

'Sl.St.' translates to 'slight stoop.'"

"And what about that *'P.S.'* comment?"

The tailor hesitated, obviously distressed. He shifted from one foot to the other and nervously rubbed his chin.

"I'd rather not say, sir, if you don't mind."

"Look--I've heard all the others and we're still friends. The *'P.S.'* surely can't be *that* bad. C'mon, let's hear it, okay?"

"As you wish, sir. *'P.S.'* means *'prominent seat.'*"

- - - - -

My most embarrassing incident, however, happened in Lima on one of our tours around South America. We were staying at the Gran Hotel Bolívar, and I had crossed the Plaza San Martín to begin a short morning stroll through the Peruvian capital.

Passing a shop along the Jirón de la Unión, an attractive bolt of suit material in a window display caught my attention. The shop was not yet open, so I made a point of returning to it later, just before completing my walk.

"¡Buenos días, señor!" exclaimed the shop owner as I entered through the heavy wrought iron door.*"¿En qué puedo servirle?"*

I indicated the cloth in the window and asked him to quote me a single-breasted two-piece suit of the material, specifying that I wanted a zipper in the trousers instead of the outmoded button fly displayed on the other suits in his store.

The price was acceptable, but he told me that I myself would have to supply the zipper--or "lightning fastener" as it is called in Spanish--since he did not stock the item in his shop. I got the centimeter measurement from him, purchased a suitable one in a nearby flea market and left it with him, after he had taken my other measurements and arranged a subsequent fitting day.

The jacket fitting was eminently satisfactory as it required only minimal alteration. I was happy all over again with my choice of material, which looked marvellous in the finished garment.

He then proudly produced the trousers and I gasped in horror. My precious zipper hit me like a slap in the face. Instead of the wretched thing being enclosed under a modest flap, as it would be in North America, it was openly brandished. It extravagantly and shamelessly exposed itself for all the street urchins to point out and snicker at.

*"Hombre, ¡por Dios!"*I remonstrated. "Such an outrage is an unexampled catastrophe. Look here,"I commanded caustically as I unzipped the slacks I was wearing. **"THIS** is the proper way to install a zipper -- *out of sight,* do you see?"

"Momento, señor." The shopkeeper went to the door of a back room and bawled, *"¡María!"* Several minutes elapsed and then out shuffled a subdued little old seamstress, timidly blinking at the sunlit windows and manifestly ill at ease.

"Look, María,"he ordered in rapid Spanish. *"This* is the way in which the *señor* wishes us to sew the lightning fastener into his pants. Study the method very carefully, María."

Immediately thereafter, as I blushingly submitted to the indignity, María inserted both bold hands into the fly of my slacks, unconcernedly teasing the material from one side to the other as she diligently satisfied herself with the placement of the zipper.

She then opened and closed the fastener repeatedly to get the hang of the thing, so to speak. All this time I was standing stock still, feeling like a country bumpkin awaiting punishment after being caught stealing apples from a neighbouring orchard.

The suit was practically perfect when I picked it up somewhat later. The embarrassment will haunt me to the end of my days.

- - - - -

For tailor-made frustration even more mind-bending however, one would be hard-pressed to match the plight of an Irish client of mine to whom I shall hereafter refer by the convenient name of <u>H</u>arold <u>C</u>asey. A name of wide renown, when you consider that its two initials can be found on <u>h</u>ot and <u>c</u>old water faucets all over the English-speaking world.

"Sure, it started with a phone call,"Casey began, certainly not in confidence, for he was still so angry that the number of folk who listened mattered not a whit. "Ye see, me friend Flanagan gets wind o' me plannin' to visit relatives in New York City.

"'Harold,' he sez on the phone, 'whoile you're there, be sure an' visit a tailor pal o'moine by the name o' McGrath, right on Fifth Avenue. He imports the foinest Oirish worsted from the ould sod, an' could give yez a rale bargain on a suit.'

"'Well, now,'thinks Oi to meself, 'Oi'll just be after doin' that,' an' sure enough whin Oi gits full o'seein' me relatives Oi goes

lookin'fer this tailor McGrath. 'Cept that he ain't at all on Fifth
Avenue, nor on Sixth, nor even on Seventh fer that matter. An'
whin Oi does catch up to him, in a hole-in-a-wall on Lexington,
he ain't the McGrath who knew me friend Flanagan neither. No,
it's his younger brother, who sez the elder McGrath's retired.
Yes, retired, an' gone outta business as well, ye see.

"But Oi looks round the brother's shop, an' spots a bit o' cloth
that catches me oye. 'Would yez make me a suit outta this?' Oi
asks. He comes over an'picks it up."That's only a remnant," he
sez, 'not enough fer a full suit. How 'bout the one *next* to it?'
Oi shakes me head.

"'Oi wouldn't wear *that* to me own *wake*,' Oi informs him.

"Well, to make a long story longer, it takes me all day to foind
a fabric which comes even close to the one Oi loiked in the first
place. He measures me an'all, jots down me name an' me ante-
cedents, then asks me to come back in siven days fer a fittin'.
By now we're both a bit frazzled, ye see, so we needs a spot o'
time to cool off.

"When Oi goes for me fittin' Oi sees the four buttons Oi wants
on each o' me sleeve cuffs, an' sure they're not there. They're
missin', fer the spalpeen has put on only three, an' these aren't
even loike the ones Oi've ordered. Besides, they're sewn on so
loosely, Oi fancies 'em fallin'off the moment Oi shakes hands
wi' a colleen or ventures a spontaneous sneeze.

"There's no trouser watch pocket, so that's missin' as well. Ye
see, Terry, Oi niver was a *wrist* person. Oi treasures that solid
ould chronometer me grandfather gave me, fob an' all, an' sure
it begs fer a proper pants pocket.

"'Ye're *dated!*' shouts McGrath whin Oi patiently explains the situation. '*Nobody* wears that koind o' watch nowadays.'

"'Then Oi guesses Oi'm a nobody,' Oi tells him, 'fer what's good enough fer me grandfather's good enough fer me.'

"'Oi'll add it in fer an extra fifty dollars,' he says.

"'Fifty dollars!'

"'Labour these days is costly,' says McGrath. 'As a matter o' fact, Oi oughtta be chargin' ye seventy-foive.'

"We reaches what the radio feller calls an *impassy.* We both argues back an' forth fer two hours, but neither budges even a half-inch. Oi calls him a filthy fifty dollar gouger an' he tells me where Oi can put me watch. Sure an' that ain't all.

"A week later Oi learns he's gotten those fabrics at a mere ten cents on the dollar, whin his brother retired. He must be makin' an obscene killin' on everythin' he palms off on a poor innocent unsuspectin' public. An unsuspectin' public which, Oi'm happy to say, *doesn't include Harold Casey!*"

--o-O-o--

TRABLER TREATS TIPPLERS

"*Aloha*, Mr. Trabler. This is Assistant Hotel Manager, Brian Thompson. Could you please come down to the front desk? We appear to have a problem in room 403."

"Oh, oh," I thought to myself. "What's it *this* time?"

"Yes, Mr. Thompson," I said into the phone, "I'll be down right away." I hung up the receiver and looked out of my ninth floor window in the Rainbow Tower of posh Hilton Hawaiian Village.

A light breeze rustled the tall coconut palms out towards the marina, and the morning sun sparkled on the sea water beyond. Savouring this idyllic scene, I dreaded confronting the problem in room 403.

As manager of a Calgary travel agency in the sixties, I was at the time escorting a 50-person tour group. The itinerary originated in Calgary, with participants flying to Vancouver, overnighting there and sailing the next afternoon on P & O liner *"Orsova"* down the Pacific coast, with stops in San Francisco and Los Angeles. The four-day sea crossing from L.A. to Honolulu had enthralled our prairie people, some of whom had never seen an ocean-going vessel except in newsreels.

Although most of our tour members were from Calgary, some resided in other cities. Our Lethbridge branch had booked three couples for instance, and several came from High River or Red Deer and other parts, as well as other provinces. One Red Deer couple, however, sorely tried our patience.

This couple, whom I shall call Ted and Sophie, had reserved just before our close-off deadline and for reasons best known to themselves, insisted on bus from Red Deer to Calgary, then rail to Vancouver. I had barely checked into the Bayshore Inn when a knock on my door revealed a visitor who turned out to be Ted from Red Deer. His clothes were rumpled, and he was sporting a black eye. Unceremoniously pushing past me, he flopped into the first available armchair to catch his breath.

"Mr. Trabler," he announced. "We haven't got our steamship tickets for Honolulu." Reaching into his inside overcoat pocket, he withdrew a flask of Alberta rye. "Care for a drink?"

"Thanks, but not right now,"I replied. "So what's this about missing steamer tickets? Our Calgary office distributed them to all of our branches ten days ago."

"Well, we didn't get ours."He took a swig from his flask and wiped his mouth on the back of his hand. He said, "Foul-up in delivery from Calgary to Red Deer, I s'pose."

"In that case," I told him, "I'll have to phone P & O's office in San Francisco and have them get you boarded on a locally-issued voucher. Where are you staying, by the way?"

"Hotel Abbotsford on Pender Street. Room 210."

"All right. Back you go to your hotel and I'll contact you first thing tomorrow morning... Now I realize it's none of my business--but if you don't mind my asking--how came you by that black eye?"

"My wife kicked me."

"I beg your pardon?"

"You see, we slept together in a lower berth on the train, for neither of us was sober enough to climb into the upper. It was a bit crowded so we slept end-to-end, and Sophie gimme a kick in the eye during the night,"Ted said matter-of-factly as though such doings were commonplace and could happen to anyone.

- - - - -

Early the following morning I phoned P & O's office in San Francisco, got clearance for Ted and Sophie to be boarded by voucher, then tried to call them at the Abbotsford. After three busy signals I decided to go there in person and give them their vouchers. I knocked on their slightly ajar hotel door, and a thin detached female voice invited me to come in.

I was unprepared for the sight that greeted me. A scantily-clad woman was doing sit-ups beside the bed.

"Where is Ted?" I inquired.

"Having breakfast in the downstairs diner," she grunted. "Oh, but you don't have to rush off, you know. Stick around, young feller... Ted won't be back for at least an hour. We could have a nice little drink together," she said with a mischievous wink.

"Thanks," I mumbled, stumbling out through the door. "I'm in a hurry today. Got a number of travel arrangements to look after between now and sailing time."

I found Ted in the downstairs cafeteria gazing glassily straight ahead as he munched a slice of dry toast. He nodded absently as he became aware of my presence.

"Here are your boarding vouchers, Ted."

"Oh," Ted recalled as he snapped out of his reverie. "We got our steamship tickets, after all. Sophie hid 'em in her tote bag so's nobody'd steal 'em on the train."

"Well, thanks a lot," I said in exasperation. "You could have phoned to tell me before I wasted so much time on alternatives."

"'S'all part o' the game," Ted remarked unconcernedly. "See yuh this afternoon on the tramp steamer."

- - - - -

In San Francisco we rode the cable car to Fisherman's Wharf and shopped at Union Square in the afternoon. Later, we did a nightclub tour which comprised Finnochio's, the Purple Onion, Bocce Ball, and a program by Louis "Satchmo"Armstrong and his combo on the Fairmont Hotel's top floor. We got back to our ship well after midnight. Ted and Sophie weren't part of that particular junket, and afterwards I found out why.

In Los Angeles we splurged on the Buena Park scenario (Disneyland and Knott's Berry Farm), Movieland Wax Museum, and outdoor lunch at the Farmer's Market.   Next day we did a Universal Studios tour and sailed for Honolulu that evening.

On the second night out from L.A. the liner's chief cabin steward came looking for me.

"Mr. Trabler, we've had a few complaints from passengers adjacent to Cabin 314. They hear loud metallic sounds from it and are unable to enjoy any sleep. Since occupants of that cabin are from your group, I'd suggest that you and I should investigate the situation."

Sure enough, it was the cabin shared by Ted and Sophie. It turned out that after ordering a case of beer, when each of them would finish a bottle he or she would toss the empty, attempting to target it to the metal trash receptacle by their night table. The resulting clang resounded the length of the corridor to the annoyance of their neighbours who sought peace and quiet.

The cabin steward and I eventually managed to get control of the predicament and the remainder of the voyage passed without further incident. As our good ship *"Orsova"* rounded Diamond Head on the fourth day, all hands assembled on deck to view the approach to the Aloha Tower, where a local choir and orchestra welcomed us with a heartwarming rendition of *"Aloha Oe."*

Our schedule called for two weeks of the Islands, the first in Waikiki with our headquarters at the Hilton Hawaiian Village complex and the second week at the Royal Lahaina Hotel on the Island of Maui. We would then fly back to Vancouver and Calgary via Canadian Pacific Airlines, as it was called at that time.

On our various sightseeing tours, Circle Island, Punchbowl, Pearl Harbor and so on, I noted that Ted and Sophie kept pretty much to themselves. They sat at the back of the bus and at each picture stop took turns debarking with the group. The one who stayed aboard, according to the driver, enjoyed a solo workout with the bottle they continually carried in their tote bag.

Their anti-social behaviour elicited no noticeable repercussions from the other tour members, although I did overhear a caustic comment or two about Ted's personal appearance, which might charitably be described as somewhat casual. So for the interim, we left them pretty much to their own resources, meanwhile on the alert to prevent any further untoward disturbance.

This calm hiatus, however, turned out to be only a lull before the inevitable storm, as subsequent events proved.

- - - - -

On our way to room 403 in the Hawaiian Village, Assistant Manager Thompson filled me in on the newest problem. Sophie had phoned the front desk asking that someone be dispatched to release Ted from their bathroom.

Apparently while Ted had been out having breakfast that morning, Sophie ordered room service to supply her with a fifth of Canadian Club, which she polished off before Ted returned.

This irked Ted to the point where he repeated the order, then took the second bottle with him into the bathroom to consume in glorious solitude, despite furious hammerings on the biffy door and unladylike, uncomplimentary epithets by Sophie.

Thompson and I, entering their room with his hotel pass key, found it in a deplorable state. Broken glass and torn-up newspapers littered the floor and furniture. Two armchairs were overturned, and window drapes hung crazily on a curtain rod suspended from a lone hook near the ceiling.

When we had got Ted out of the bathroom and ready to listen to reason, I said, "When you come right down to it, this trip isn't really what you expected, eh, Ted?"

"Nope, it shore ain't. But the whole dang deal was Sophie's idea, not mine, since the very beginning."

"In fact, all you've done on it so far you could have just as easily done in your own kitchen in Red Deer, right?"

"Right. And without half the hassle."

So I persuaded him to accompany me by taxicab to Canadian Pacific's office on Kalakaua Avenue. He'd a three-day growth of beard, his tie was outside his collar on the left and inside on the right, and his crumpled serge suit looked as though he had slept in a sauna. As we were getting out of the taxicab at our destination, the driver alerted Ted that his fly was undone.

I explained to the airline clerk that Ted and Sophie needed to change their reservations to return home that very evening and would not continue their tour as planned. They'd also cancel their rail tickets between Vancouver and Calgary, and go by air instead. The clerk made the necessary amendments and I can still see his eyes bug out when Ted, despite his scruffy *façade*, produced a wad of thousand dollar bills to cover the charges.

That evening like a mother hen, I carefully escorted Ted and Sophie downstairs to board a cab to the airport.

"Where's the rest of your luggage?" I asked, noting they had only their tote bags with them.

"We sent it on out to the airport," Ted informed me. "Shore will be nice to get back to lil' ol' Red Deer!"

I had meanwhile cabled our Red Deer office to advise them of developments. Only then did they give me the background on our two terrible tipplers. Just before booking the tour Sophie had been diagnosed with leukemia by her physician. He'd told her she had approximately six months to live. Sophie stoically received this piece of news and immediately decided she'd go out in a blaze rather than a fizzle.

Back in my hotel room that evening, I felt as though a great load had been lifted from my shoulders. Looking at my watch, I realized that Ted and Sophie had now been airborne for two hours and were halfway to Vancouver. The telephone rang.

"It's the downstairs bell captain, Mr. Trabler. What are we supposed to do with this Red Deer baggage that was left with us early in the afternoon?"

--o-O-o--

TRABLER VOLUNTEERS VARIETY

"Since you're visiting Hawaii for the first time," I told him, "you should make an effort to get an overall idea of the various islands. In that way you'll intelligently decide which of them you prefer, and on your next trip you'll spend more of it at that particular destination."

"Can't I just head for one island and stay there until it's time to come back home?"

"Of course you can, Mr. Kane. But each island has its own characteristics. You'd be cheating yourself if you didn't make a point of comparing them for your own satisfaction. I've seen people spend their entire holiday in just Honolulu for example, and then complain about it being only another big city and far too commercialized for holiday enjoyment."

"I think I see what you mean."

"On the other hand, we've had cases where people tried to cover all the islands in one short week, and came home utterly confused and exhausted."

"So what do you feel I should do in *my* situation?"

"Well, before we make any fast decisions, suppose you tell me how long a period you have at your disposal."

My name is Terry Trabler. I own and manage a chain of travel agencies. The episode I relate happened long ago, but its relevance is just as valid today as it was back then.

The travel industry, steadily growing more complicated and competitive, has lost some of its early appeal, especially for the patient souls who attempt to update their clients on its multiple changes. These patient souls are the overworked and underpaid travel agents in whose ranks I rejoiced, reacted, rebelled and re-searched for over thirty hectic years.

Not many contemporary occupations are hassle-free, even beneath the umbrella of sophisticated technology. Automation, originally posing as a cure-all, has latterly spawned an upsurge of professional trouble-shooters, whose pet recommendation is time management. This is a misnomer because nobody literally manages time. One manages only oneself in relation to the time available. This spins off into the much-quoted adage that losers count time while winners make time count.

But let's get back to the episode in question. It began with a request for additional information on a package vacation which our agency had been pushing for several weeks. The inquiring gentleman, a rather withdrawn individual whom I shall call Ron Kane, dropped into our main branch during his lunch break.

"I saw your ad in this morning's *Herald*," he remarked in an apologetic manner, "and as I am the only one in our office who has not been to Hawaii, I feel it's time I had a first-hand look at this Paradise they're always talking about." He blinked a couple of times and cleared his throat nervously.

"Nothing compares with seeing a place for oneself," I agreed, trying to put him at ease. "Few things are more annoying than overhearing talk about unfamiliar territory."

"Well," he nodded, "it *does* put one at a disadvantage."

"Now, Mr. Kane," I continued, "you say you've never been to Hawaii. I take it, though, that you've travelled to a few other places. Am I right?"

"Not really," he confided. "I'm afraid I'm what they call a drudge, a stick-in-the-mud, and any vacations I've taken before were right here in the city, just catching up on my long overdue personal correspondence."

"And which," I reminded him, "in all honesty were scarcely holidays at all."

"I guess you're right, Mr. Trabler."

"So now it's time we arranged something sufficiently removed from your usual routine as to be truly recreational."

I got out the Hawaiian package brochure and we went over it together, as I outlined all the optional side-trips, meal plans, car rental procedures and choices of accommodation. Then it came to what period of time he could afford.

"I believe I could spare a month, Mr. Trabler."

"All right then. With that much time, I would recommend a week each on Oahu, Kauai, Maui, and the big Island of Hawaii. That will allow a long enough stay to get the *feel* of each."

"Before we settle it, could you give me a brief rundown on the islands you've mentioned, one at a time?"

"Certainly, Mr. Kane. They have a fascinating history from the arrival of the first Polynesian outriggers to their assumption of

American statehood, in 1959. The current population is a mixture of Asian, Polynesian, European and American peoples."

"I've read that Captain Cook called Hawaii 'Sandwich Islands' after the Earl of Sandwich in England."

"Right, but somehow that name didn't take. Maybe the natives visualize their spread as a full meal rather than just a sandwich. Now, the four I outlined are the largest of a group of eight. The island of Oahu (Hawaiian for *"gathering place"*) is the site of Honolulu, the state's capital. It likewise contains such famous places as Pearl Harbor, Diamond Head, and Iolani Palace (King Kalakaua played billiards and poker in its basement). Other interesting places are the Nuuanu-Pali cliff, the Sea Life Park, and the Polynesian Cultural Center."

"Excuse me, Mr. Trabler. One of our staff said something about a free cruise around Pearl Harbor. Was he joking?"

"Not at all. The U.S. Navy operates it. The only drawback is that, because it is free, you may have to stand several hours in a lineup before leaving the pier. Should that possibility not appeal to you, there are Honolulu tour outfits who do charge a fee but get you there in jig time. Whichever category you opt for you'll see the sunken hulls of battleships Arizona and Utah. You can actually go aboard the Arizona memorial and read the names of the men who died in action."

"Thanks. Now, what about the other islands?"

"Okay. The next would be Kauai, the Garden Isle, which was the film location for *'South Pacific.'* You can explore Kauai's Wailua River by motor launch right to the Fern Grotto."

"The Fern Grotto. Seems to me a couple from our office went there to get married."

"I wouldn't be surprised. Word gets around, because it's a very beautiful location for a wedding. You can also relax at Hanalei and Poipu Beaches, view the Waimea Canyon by helicopter, or enjoy thousands of sweet-scented flowers. Geologically, Kauai is the oldest of the islands, and certainly the lushest."

"Several of my friends seem to prefer Maui. What are a few of its highlights and which of them should I see first?"

"Maui, the Valley Isle, is formed by two linked volcanoes and Lahaina, former capital of the Hawaiian Kingdom, was the site of many 19th century fights between whalers and missionaries."

"Oh, yes. I remember reading something about that in a book by James Michener."

"So here I try in my own poor manner to describe the islands when you're already brainwashed by the masterful Michener!"

"Not really, Mr. Trabler. I read the book years ago, and I'm afraid I've forgotten a lot of it, except certain things that come back to me when I'm reminded of them."

"Well anyway, he undoubtedly mentioned Mt. Haleakala, the world's widest volcano. Huge cinder cones on its 19-mile-wide floor can be seen from the House of the Sun Observatory, some 10,000 feet up on the edge of the crater, or you could explore them on foot or by horse."

"I'm not sure I'd want to do that, Mr. Trabler. You see, I have respiratory problems, and a 10,000 foot altitude would certainly aggravate my condition."

"I understand. Still, you could get your doctor's opinion and be guided accordingly."

"Thanks, that's just what I would do for sure. Okay, in case he prescribes my staying at ground level, what else can I see?"

"Well now, in the Kipahulu Valley you'll find many rare birds, some spectacular waterfalls, and the Seven Sacred Pools. There is an ancient sugar mill near the Royal Lahaina Hotel. The Hale Hoikeke museum, in Wailuku, contains hundreds of silver and wooden Hawaiian artifacts. Also, both the Kaanapali and Kihei areas have excellent reasonably-priced golf courses."

"Shucks, Mr. Trabler. To me the golf scene would be a waste. I'm a dyed-in-the-wool duffer in any sports. But you mentioned another island I think you called the Big Island of Hawaii. What attractions does that one have?"

"Hawaii is geologically the youngest. It's famous for its fiery volcanoes and its wide variety of beautiful orchids."

"Excuse me. Did you say orchids?"

"Yes. The Big Island is known as the Orchid Isle. It also has black sand beaches on its Kona coast and many macadamia nut processing plants. And its Parker cattle ranch is huge, one of the world's largest, in fact."

"Okay, thanks for all the information. Now, I see that my lunch hour is nearly over, so could you please give me some of your pamphlets to study at home this evening? Then as soon as I've reached a decision I'll come back and make my booking."

I could see there was no point in pressing for a definite commitment at that particular time, so I handed him several of our miscellaneous Hawaiian brochures and he was on his way.You don't rush someone like Mr. Kane -- any slight pressure would spook him and he would gallop off like a skittish palomino.

All in all, though, I figured I had given him sufficient description, both in words and literature, to enable him to reach an intelligent decision. I could visualize him poring over the folders and pestering his colleagues at the office.

A week went by. The telephone rang.

"Travel with Trabler, good morning!" answered my secretary Cindy with her usual customer-oriented cheerfulness. "Yes, he is right here... may I tell him who's calling?"

"It's for you, Terry. A Mr. Ronald Kane from Consolidated Accounting Services across the way."

"Thanks, Cindy... Good morning, Mr. Kane!"

"Sorry to trouble you, Mr. Trabler, but I was wondering if you could send me a brochure about the island of Molokai. I don't seem to have anything on it in what you gave me last week."

"No problem, Mr. Kane. I shall drop it in the mail to you this afternoon, to your office or your home, whichever you prefer. Do you have any questions about the literature you have been studying since your visit?"

"Not really, but one of the folders mentioned a Father Damien who apparently lived on Molokai at the leper colony."

"That's right, and his dedication to the inmates was so intense that he contracted leprosy himself and died of it."

"So I'm told. I understand that the colony no longer exists and the island is now being developed as the newest resort by some of the tour companies."

"That's right, Mr. Kane. And because of that very factor it still preserves more of the original Hawaiian lifestyle than you'll see on the other more sophisticated islands."

"In that case, Mr. Trabler, if I decide to visit Molokai as one of my four, which of the others should I eliminate?"

"Well, Mr. Kane, the choice would really be yours, although I feel with so much to see on the big island of Hawaii, maybe you could postpone visiting that one for a later trip. But please don't be influenced by what is, after all, only my own opinion."

"Thanks for your help, Mr. Trabler. I'll call you back."

When he eventually did, it was to notify us that, as there were so many hard decisions to make and as he again had to catch up on a great deal of personal correspondence, he probably would not travel for another year.

We win some and we lose some!

--o-O-o--

TRABLER WHEELS AND DEALS

"You say I can't book a promenade deck stateroom on your March Caribbean cruise?" I sputtered into the phone, suddenly flattened by this unexpected turn of events. "How about bridge deck?"

"Not a chance," the ship's reservations person replied. "The entire sailing has been sold out for weeks."

"Thanks, anyway," I growled, "guess I'll have to talk to your competitors." I hung up the phone and buzzed my secretary.

"Cindy," I said as she appeared, "did you know that Fantastic Cruise Lines have completely filled their March sailing?"

"Well, no," she replied. "I haven't been speaking to them lately. But I'm not surprised, the way they've been flogging it like crazy through the media."

"Right, and they put on that special extravaganza last month at the Misadventure Inn. People turned out for it who had never in their stay-at-home lives even *thought* of a cruise."

"The same people who were ripe to be won over by the Fantastic sales-reps' hardhitting now-or-never pitch,"Cindy agreed, as she riffled through our scrapbook of suppliers' ads.

"But not the type for whom I'm trying to book space on that particular sailing," I reflected. "I should have recognized all the danger signals much earlier. Cindy, this calls for some serious step-by-step strategic planning."

"What would you like me to do?" she asked, with her *déjà vu* oh, oh, here-we-go-again look plainly showing.

"For starters, you could phone all tour package operators to ascertain how many unsold staterooms they've got blocked off on that date," I suggested. "Then give me the numbers and I'll take it from there. I'll need half a dozen cabins at least."

Actually, I told myself, I really shouldn't get involved in this type of deal. It would mean splitting commissions with each wholesaler, which, depending on their individual policies, was frequently difficult or impossible, besides being theoretically illegal. Revenue watchdogs took a dim view of that brand of profit-sharing. Still, the ever-growing dog-eat-dog nature of the industry made it necessary to resort to such measures if an agency were to survive. Nobody liked it but everybody did it.

The booking I had tried to make was a family get-together for six couples, four aunts and uncles and two sets of cousins who wanted to travel *en masse* on the same ship. All of them were loyal clients of our agency. Unfortunately they had taken a bit too long to reach their final decision, but were still counting on our customary promptness and efficiency, so something would have to be done, and quickly.

Later that afternoon, Cindy told me that Funseeker Holiday Packages had a pending cancellation of a six-stateroom block for the sailing in question.

"Wonderful!" I sighed with relief. "There's a ray of sunshine after all. Any idea of which agency is involved?"

"As a matter of fact," Cindy murmured, "your ever-diligent

secretary through devious ways accidentally discovered it probably could be Keating Travel down the street."

"That makes it even better," I observed. "So would you please phone their manager Mike Johnson for me, Cindy?"

"Mike," I began, when he came on the line, "I hear via the grapevine that you may have to cancel a block of six staterooms on Fantastic's March cruise."

"Bad news travels fast, eh, Terry? Yeah, there's nothing one can do about a death in the family. It does happen."

"Have you notified the supplier yet, Mike?"

"I'm just getting around to it. What do you have in mind?"

"I could use the space, and I wondered if we might work out some sort of deal before it gets thrown to the wolves."

"Won't be easy, Terry. Names and passport numbers already were registered with the shipping people. In addition, once the space is released, it automatically goes to the standby names at the top of the waitlist. You know that as well as I do. Fair's fair, old man, and we'd both holler loud enough if someone tried to pull that kind of partiality on either of *us*."

"Correct, Mike. But circumstances alter cases. I have a gut reaction that Funseekers could do with a bit of extra business to make up for that charter cancellation they had last month. And if I approach them in the right way I believe they'll listen."

"Well, hop to it, Terry. I'll hang on to the space merely long enough for you to do your finagling with Funseekers. But just get back to me as soon as possible, eh?"

"Okay, Mike; you have my word you'll not get left holding the hazard. Incidentally, were your people sold insurance?"

"You got that right, Terry. Nobody but nobody travels through this office without it. Too many emergencies can happen."

"I figured so, but just wanted to be sure." We hung up and I immediately phoned Funseekers.

"Is Bill Davis there?" I asked the receptionist who answered. "He is," she replied. "May I tell him who's calling?"

"You may. It's Terry from Travel with Trabler."

"Good afternoon, Terry." Bill's booming voice reverberated in the receiver, which I instinctively distanced from my head in order to protect my ear drum. "How may I help you?"

"I'll come right to the point, Bill. First let me say how sorry we all were to hear about your ill-fated charter. That kind of setback hurts the whole industry. You have our sympathy."

"Thanks, Terry, we're still licking our wounds, but it's not the end of the world. We're just a little hungrier, that's all."

"So perhaps a six-block package of cruise staterooms at this juncture wouldn't be entirely unwelcome," I suggested.

"Are you serious?" he asked cautiously, after what seemed an eternity of stunned silence.

"Bill, you know I never kid the troops. The booty is waiting if you want it, and one big chunk is more agreeable than a lot of little dribs and drabs, right?"

"Tell me more, Terry. I can do with a magic windfall."

"Fine. To begin with, I'm talking about a parcel that is in need of recycling, because of a sudden death in a family. Are you still interested, or should I be phoning someone else?"

"Hold on there, Terry. Don't let's jump to conclusions before we've heard the whole story, okay? Let's have the details."

"All right, Bill. I have a family group of six couples, four uncles and aunts and two sets of cousins, who wish to cruise *en famille* on Fantastic's March sailing to the Caribbean. As you may or may not know, that particular sailing has been sold out for several weeks."

"I wasn't aware of that. Please go on."

"I have it on good authority that another agency (no names, no pack drill) is about to surrender a same-sized block of space due to a recent decease. At this late date it would be difficult to resell that space piecemeal, so I'm offering to save the day for you, by supplying twelve warm live bodies to occupy those six staterooms. Is it a deal, Bill?"

"Now just a doggone minute, Terry. Are you telling me that Funseekers already have some involvement?"

"Exactly. Funseekers sold the original package and are about to see it dumped back in their lap. But as I've said, we can get you out of a bad jam if you're willing to coöperate."

"Terry, you old fox. You've got me over a barrel and you know it. Just the same, I don't particularly relish a transaction like this. It's not strictly legal, you know."

"That's true. But we're both aware that it's being done all the time, right? So instead of working your tails off trying to resell those six cabins in bits and pieces and perhaps getting stuck with one or two at the deadline, you can accept my offer of a fine full package and come out smelling like a rose."

"What about commission?"

"You'll automatically get your usual ten per cent, Bill, and I'll negotiate a mutually satisfactory arrangement with the other agency. That way no one takes a beating and everyone's happy."

"And what do we do about the names and passport numbers that are already registered with the shipping line?"

"In checking with the other agency I found they had insisted on cancellation insurance, which has a specific death clause in its coverage. As a result, there can be a wholesale revision of names without it being contested by the authorities."

"Well Terry, it sounds as though you've done your homework on this one...You folks have always had an excellent reputation in the industry, as well as constantly being our top producer. So I don't mind telling you if anyone else offered me a similar deal I wouldn't touch it with a ten-metre totem pole, and I mean that most sincerely. If it's not too classified, may I ask which other agency is in the picture?"

"Sorry, Bill, but you understand I'm not at liberty to disclose that until I've got *their* okay as well. In any case, I promise to get back to you the moment they agree to the terms you and I have just discussed. Any other questions?"

"No, I think you've plugged all the holes. And I'll repeat what I said before. We can sure use the business."

My secretary Cindy was at my elbow as I hung up the phone. "Your client Mr. Abercrombie is holding for you on line three," she confided. "He sounds just a bit perturbed."

"Oh, oh," I thought, "What now?" Fred Abercrombie was senior spokesman of the family group for whom I was doing the wheeling and dealing between Keating and Funseekers.

"Good afternoon, Fred," I said, after pushing the button for line three. "Sorry if I've kept you waiting."

"No problem, Terry," he assured me. "But I'm afraid I've got some disappointing news for you."

"Break it to me gently, Fred. This day hasn't been altogether promising thus far and it's not nearly over."

"Already you're making me feel bad. I only wanted to say we'll have to postpone our Caribbean cruise until the fall. Our family G.P. has advised my wife Sadie that she urgently needs surgery and must have a few weeks to recuperate afterwards."

This information hit me like a load of anvils. Here was my careful planning wasted. Tossed in a wastebasket as if it didn't matter in the slightest. I sat in shocked silence.

"Hello, *hello*?" Fred's voice reached me again. "Terry, are you still there? That's not all I have to tell you."

"You mean there's worse to come?" I murmured haltingly.

"Now, now! I merely wanted to let you know that my young brother Henry and family have volunteered to fill in for us and take over our reservation for the six staterooms, as long as it's not too much trouble for you at this late date."

"No trouble at all, Fred." I was back on track and breathing a lot more freely. "Could you please give me the new names?"

--o-O-o--

TRABLER YIELDS TO A YEARNING

Sooner or later it had to happen.

Every now and then, during my many long years in the travel business, I would say to myself, "Won't it be nice when I can sit back and let someone else number the noses, count the carry-ons, label the luggage, jolly the jaded, soothe the sufferers, and manage the myriad matters required of a tour escort!"

When my retirement date finally arrived, therefore, I'd already made up my mind to do two things to bolster my declining years. I joined the Canadian Authors Association so as to devote a little more time to the casual writing I had been doing before in my spare moments. I also accepted an invitation for membership in Victoria's prestigious Arion Male Voice Choir, founded in 1892.

These two activities, I felt, would keep me mentally active and permit me to wear out rather than rust out, as the saying goes. It was through the Arion Choir that I finally earned the opportunity to realize my dream of letting someone else be tour escort.

For fifty years Arion had traditionally done joint concerts with the Eugene Gleemen of Oregon, alternating between Eugene and Victoria every two or three seasons. Both choirs sang an eclectic mix of selections, ranging from anthems to Broadway show tune medleys, renowned folk songs, Gilbert & Sullivan, grand opera, Negro spirituals and London music hall favourites.

During my presidential year with Arion, the Eugene Gleemen invited my wife and myself to accompany them on a concert tour of southern Germany and Austria, where we were to perfom nine concerts over a two-week period.

Arriving in Frankfurt, we were taken by two elegant Mercedes-Benz buses to Mainz and Bacharach, where we boarded the Köln-Düsseldorf steamer for a short cruise down the Rhine. Sailing by a famous promontory, we gathered on deck and sang, in German, *"Die Lorelei,"* enthusiastically aided by the vessel's other passengers and crew who, of course, had known this folk song by heart since early childhood.

"A rare, once-in-a-lifetime thrill," decided one of the Gleemen, when we later assembled in the ship's dining room for lunch. "It was worth the price of our trip just to see the joy and appreciation on the faces of the locals when we sang that song."

At Boppard we reboarded our buses for St. Wendel, where we were met by the families who had long since volunteered to host us for the ensuing three nights. My wife and I stayed with Günter and Siegrid Baltes and their teenage son and daughter. They took us in and treated us even better than if we had been relatives.

The following day, Saturday, saw us on a walking tour of Trier, Germany's oldest city. It had just observed the two thousandth anniversary of its founding by the Romans. Our tour included a visit to the Roman baths, where we marvelled over the intricate construction, particularly the stark, severe underground quarters provided for the stokers who heated the bath water.

"Poor, unfortunate devils," commented one of our group. "Just imagine living and working all your life in a hell-hole like this!"

"Guess they had no choice," said another. "In those days there were no unions, you know."

"Unions wouldn't have made much difference, because all the workers in this section were undoubtedly indentured slaves."

After two concerts, one in Trier and one in Tholey's venerable abbey, and a *wunderbar* banquet with our homestay host families, we proceeded to Heidelberg and put on an impromptu program in that city's famous castle.

"But we didn't see the stupid prince!" complained the wife of one of our number immediately afterward.

"You mean the *student* prince, don't you?" said her husband.

"Not at all,"she replied. "He *must* have been stupid, because in the musical he never did marry that nice Kathy waitress girl."

Continuing up the Neckar Valley to Bad Rappenau, we did an afternoon performance before moving on to Stuttgart. Our two days in Stuttgart included a tour of the Mercedes-Benz factory and an evening concert at Winnenden. Following lunch next day in Nördlingen we took the "Romantic Road" to Fussen to trudge uphill through a heavy downpour to the Neuschwanstein Castle (upon which the Disneyland replica is modelled), then onward to Schwangau. There we spent the evening drying our clothes and shoes, still sopping wet due to the castle episode.

Our Schwangau hotel was named *König Ludwig*, after the so-called "mad"King Ludwig of Bavaria who nearly fiscally ruined the country, in his zeal for financing elaborate castle homes like the Neuschwanstein. On our way to Oberammergau the ensuing day we visited another of his pet palaces called the Linderhof.

We shopped all over Oberammergau (where the Passion Play is

held every ten years) and went by lovely Garmisch-Partenkirchen
to Salzburg for two nights in the Hotel Humboldt, and where we
got to sing in the Cathedral. Mozart's home town of Salzburg is
relatively close to the Berchtesgaden salt mines, which have been
operating for over six centuries. At the mines, we were all issued
baggy coveralls to protect our clothing while we descended to the
underground brine lake, considerably over 2,700 metres beneath
the earth's surface.

"This lake," our guide told us, "results from many hundreds of
years' pumping down water to absorb the salt from the rock formations. The brine, of course, is then pumped to the surface where
the salt is extracted by condensation and crystallized."

We crossed the lake on a huge raft, and on the other side were
transported by elevator back to the entrance, and photographed in
our baggy coveralls as a memento for the folks at home.

"After having consumed vast quantities," remarked a wiseacre
in the crowd, "of *Wienerschnitzel, Bratwurst, Leberknödelsuppe,
Apfel Strudel,* and *Schwarzwälder Kirschtorte,* I can understand
the wisdom of these baggy garments. They're a charitable cover-
up for our overindulgence!"

Between Salzburg and München a ferry ride got us to another
Ludwig castle, the "Herrenchiemsee" in the middle of a lake.

In München we sang for a huge and very appreciative audience
that had gathered for the noonday clock ceremony in the townhall
square of Marienplatz. Following several more concerts and visits
to cities like Nüremberg, Dachau, Ingolstadt, Bamberg, Pommers-
felden and Rothenburg (where we sang beneath the famed "Drinking Clock") we wound up at Ladenberg for our farewell dinner.

It was during this farewell dinner that a heartwarming incident took place. One of the Gleemen rose to his feet and made a short speech about how glad their organization was to be accompanied on their tour by two congenial Canadians. Immediately afterward they all got up and sang *"O Canada!"* especially for us. We were speechless and understandably moved.

Still and all, the icing on the cake was for this old codger to be able to sit back and finally let someone else escort the tour!

GLOSSARY OF FOREIGN TERMS IN ORDER OF OCCURRENCE*

(Numbers refer to book pages)

1. *Cinco más cuatro por nueve menos uno entre ocho* = "Five plus four times nine minus one divided by eight."
¿Cuánto son? = "How much?"
¡Señor Jackson! = "Mr. Jackson!"
Son diez, señor Profesor = "The answer is ten, teacher."

2. *tapatía* = native of Guadalajara.
Restaurante del Lago = "Restaurant by the Lake."

3. *canadiense* = Canadian.   *inglés* = English.

4. *concienzudamente* = thoroughly.   *mi corazón* = my heart.
con quien = with whom.   *querido* = dear, beloved.
mi familia = my family.   *¿entiendes?* = "you understand?"

7. *La Fuente* = "The Fountain."

8. *guacamole* = spicy avocado salad.

10. *protégés* = people promoted by influential persons.
hors d'oeuvres = appetizers.

30. *Hotel das Cataratas* = "Waterfalls Hotel."
Carnaval = Latin-American *"Mardi Gras"* celebration.

36. *Libiamo ne' lieti* = "A bumper we'll drain" *(La Traviata)*
Caro nome che il mio cor = "Dear name within this breast"
                                                     (Rigoletto)

* Omitting those already translated in the text.

37. *amico Pietro* = "Friend Peter."
    è il mio compleanno = "It's my birthday."

38. *Conosco dei giuochi da adulti* = "I know some grown-up games."
    dolce tesoro = honeybunch.
    reggisseno scollato = cut-away bra.
    mutandine trasparenti = see-through panties.

50. *mariachis* = Mexican street singers and musicians.
    Ballet Folklórico = Folkloric Ballet (a Mexican creation).
    Jarabe Tapatío = Music for the traditional Mexican hat
                       dance, Guadalajara style.

51. *blasé* = uninterested or unexcited because of frequent ex-
             posure or indulgence. Also "very sophisticated."
             (French past participle of *blaser*, to cloy.)

69. *maestro* = music composer, conductor, or teacher.

88. *señor* = sir, or Mister. (sometimes "gentleman.")

89. *à la* = in the manner or style of.

91. *faux pas* = a social blunder.
    Noble Patria, etc. = "Noble fatherland! Your handsome
                           flag portrays your life to us; under
            your clear blue sky, peace rests fair and pure."

92. *En estómago vacío, etc.* = "Nobility of soul does not fill
                                 an empty stomach."

96. *cheongsam* = an Oriental type side-slit skirt.
    sampan = a flat-bottomed Oriental skiff moved by oars.

98. *macho* = ostensibly male.

99. *¡Buenos días, señor!* = "Good morning, sir!"
    ¿En qué puedo servirle? = "How may I help you?"

100. *Hombre, ¡por Dios!* = "Good Heavens, man!"
     Momento, señor = "Just a moment, sir."
     the *señor* = "the gentleman." (See p. 88)

104. *Aloha* = "Hello" in this case. Can also mean "goodbye,"
     "love," "here's how!" (as a toast)

108. *Aloha Oe* = "Farewell to You," most famous of the more
     than 200 songs composed by Liliuokalani,
     last Queen of Hawaii, 1838-1917.

129. *Die Lorelei* = German folk song, based on a legend of a
     beautiful woman who sings on a steep rock
     by the Rhine, above Coblenz, luring sailors
     to their death on the rocks below.

130. *wunderbar* = wonderful, marvellous.

131. *Wienerschnitzel* = veal cutlet.   *Bratwurst* = sausage
     for frying. *Leberknödelsuppe* = liver and noodle soup.
     Apfel Strudel = apple strudel.   *Schwarzwälder Kirsch-*
     torte = Black Forest cherry cake.

THE END

ISBN 1553697103

9 781553 697107